S0-CBT-009

"Remember when we went to that carnival and got stuck on the Ferris wheel?"

Evie chuckled. "Don't act like that was a rare occurrence. I think everyone in Bishop's Gate has gotten stuck on that Ferris wheel one time or another."

"I won't deny that. Still—do you remember the night it was our turn?"

"Absolutely. I remember that it was pretty much the hottest night of the year."

It *had* been hot. Evie had worn short jean shorts, blistering-white Keds and a bright teal halter top. She'd been all smooth, tan skin and golden hair. Gorgeous. "You were the only girl who didn't panic when the wind picked up and our seat started rocking."

Evie leaned closer, her bare arm brushing against his…just as it had so long ago. "That's because I was the only girl who had August Meyer's arm around her."

Dear Reader,

I loved writing *The Good Mother!* The characters in this book made me smile. Evie—the divorced mom with a healthy sense of duty and humor. August—the guy who looks like a model and has heaps of integrity. I liked Evie's daughter, Jenna, every bossy, demanding four feet of her. And I loved Evie's dad—who likes to run and smoke cigars…all at the same time. Each is the kind of person I'd like to meet and certainly go on vacation with!

However, the main reason I liked writing this book so much is that it takes place in the summer and I wrote it all during the winter. I brought a little space heater into my office and placed it right by my feet… and began to think about beach cottages and Ferris wheels. Summer crushes and snow cones. Corn dogs and sand in between my toes. As you can imagine, the days flew by!

I finished *The Good Mother* during an ice storm. For three days we had no school, the roads were treacherous to drive on and every tree in our yard tilted forlornly toward the ground, heavy from the weight of ice. Between bouts of popcorn, hot chocolate and games of Life, I'd dart back to my make-believe world of Bishop's Gate and dream of suntans and romance.

I hope you enjoy *The Good Mother* as much as I enjoyed writing it. And maybe as we head toward fall and winter and the days get shorter, you, too, might look forward to a trip to the coast of Florida, where the sky is sunny, the family is wonderful and rekindled love is in the air.

Shelley

The Good Mother

SHELLEY GALLOWAY

HARLEQUIN®

TORONTO • NEW YORK • LONDON
AMSTERDAM • PARIS • SYDNEY • HAMBURG
STOCKHOLM • ATHENS • TOKYO • MILAN • MADRID
PRAGUE • WARSAW • BUDAPEST • AUCKLAND

If you purchased this book without a cover you should be aware that this book is stolen property. It was reported as "unsold and destroyed" to the publisher, and neither the author nor the publisher has received any payment for this "stripped book."

ISBN-13: 978-0-373-75187-7
ISBN-10:   0-373-75187-7

THE GOOD MOTHER

Copyright © 2007 by Shelley Sabga.

All rights reserved. Except for use in any review, the reproduction or utilization of this work in whole or in part in any form by any electronic, mechanical or other means, now known or hereafter invented, including xerography, photocopying and recording, or in any information storage or retrieval system, is forbidden without the written permission of the publisher, Harlequin Enterprises Limited, 225 Duncan Mill Road, Don Mills, Ontario M3B 3K9, Canada.

This is a work of fiction. Names, characters, places and incidents are either the product of the author's imagination or are used fictitiously, and any resemblance to actual persons, living or dead, business establishments, events or locales is entirely coincidental.

This edition published by arrangement with Harlequin Books S.A.

® and TM are trademarks of the publisher. Trademarks indicated with ® are registered in the United States Patent and Trademark Office, the Canadian Trade Marks Office and in other countries.

www.eHarlequin.com

Printed in U.S.A.

ABOUT THE AUTHOR

Shelley Galloway loves to get up early, drink too much coffee and write books. These pastimes come in handy during her day-to-day life in southern Ohio. Most days she can be found driving her kids to their activities, writing romances in her basement or trying to find a way to get ahead of her pile of laundry. She's also been known to talk to her miniature dachshund, Suzy, as if she actually has opinions about books.

Shelley is the proud recipient of a *Romantic Times BOOKclub* Reviewer's Choice Award for her 2006 release, *Simple Gifts*. Shelley attends several conferences every year and loves to meet readers. She also spends a lot of time online. Please visit her at eHarlequin.com or at www.shelleygalloway.com.

Books by Shelley Galloway

HARLEQUIN AMERICAN ROMANCE

Don't miss any of our special offers. Write to us at the following address for information on our newest releases.

Harlequin Reader Service
U.S.: 3010 Walden Ave., P.O. Box 1325, Buffalo, NY 14269
Canadian: P.O. Box 609, Fort Erie, Ont. L2A 5X3

To Tom.
Back when we met, my accent was thicker,
my figure was better and wrinkles around my eyes
were only something to dread. Thanks for making
me still feel like the girl you fell in love with…
all those years ago.

Chapter One

In her next life, Evie was going to think things through just a little bit more carefully. Think about things like good old cause and effect.

Brrrinnnggg! Bring, breeng! Bringgg!

Case in point. How come she hadn't considered just how terrible the shrill ring of a fake cell phone would sound in her baby daughter's hands when she was in Grab-A-Lot Dollar Store two days ago? Thinking ahead would have done her a lot of good.

Briinnggg!

"Momma, make Missy stop! Her stupid cell phone is drivin' me crazy!"

Leave it to Jenna to tell it like it was.

"Missy, stop," Evie said, more to please her seven-year-old than to bring about any change in her toddler.

Jenna had never been one to suffer fools, or to suffer her baby sister's needs and wishes. Actually, from the moment her little redheaded darling had been born, she hadn't been in the mood to put up with much of anything, which was really too bad, since Evie could have used some support at the moment.

Briiinnnngggg!

"Momma! She's not stopping."

A better mother would be more patient and kind. But Jenna had come about her personality rightfully…which meant a lot of the time Evie didn't have much patience, either. "Thanks for the update."

"Can't you do something?"

"No, and you can't, either. Don't touch that phone," she added, when she heard Jenna shifting closer to the baby, which could only mean the toy was about to be snatched.

It didn't take a genius to know what would happen then. Missy screaming—loud, clear and unrelenting.

"But Momma—"

"Don't touch it."

Breeeinnngggg! Bring! Ding!

"I hate that phone! Can I at least say that?"

"You may." Evie drummed her fingers on her steering wheel and hoped she was going to make it to her parents' without going crazy or wondering yet again why she'd decided to make the drive from Texas to Florida's panhandle in two days.

After all, the girls were acting just like all the parenting books said they were supposed to. Jenna was all of seven and trying so hard to be helpful, even if she was only helping to benefit herself. Missy was just a baby.

As the toy rang and whistled and Jenna sighed dramatically, Evie glanced up to meet her eldest's glare in the rearview mirror. "Why don't you color or something?"

Out went the lip. "I'm sick of coloring. And I can't do anything with Missy going nuts with that phone."

"It's keeping her happy. Look on the bright side. She's not crying."

"Well, *I'm* not happy."

Evie wasn't, either, but since no one had cared about

that during the last year, she didn't bother to bring it up now. "You're just going to have to be patient."

"How much longer until we get to Bishop's Gate?"

Recalling that they'd just passed the sign for I-85, Evie guesstimated they were close. "One hour. Maybe less." Bishop's Gate was a sleepy little beachside town on the west coast of Florida. As the resort billboards on the side of the road advertised, nonstop fun was just minutes away.

Jenna groaned like that was an eternity. "Momma, we've been in here forever."

"Only nine hours."

"I don't see why we had to vacation in Florida, anyway."

"I told you why. We're going to Bishop's Gate because it's where I vacationed every summer when I was a little girl."

"Now Missy and me get to go."

It was truly amazing just how sarcastic a seven-year-old could be. "Yep." And they were going to have a *fun* time.

"Daddy said Gulf Shores was closer."

"Daddy's not here." Evie winced as she heard her sharp tone. Because she promised herself never to talk bad about John in the girls' presence, Evie added, "Don't forget, Grandma and Grandpa will be at the house when we get there. We're going to grill hot dogs tonight, then all go to the beach tomorrow."

As Missy pressed another three buttons on the phone and squealed with laughter, Jenna folded her arms across her chest, a true imitation of her father. "Daddy's going to be all alone while we're in Florida for one whole month."

Evie seriously doubted that. Ever since their divorce, John had spent very little time home alone. In fact, he'd spent very little time "finding himself," which was what he'd said he needed to do the night he'd said their marriage was over.

But that wasn't something good mothers told their

daughters. "We'll call Daddy tomorrow. You can tell him all about the trip. You're going to send him pictures, too, remember?"

"I remember." As Missy kicked her pudgy legs against the navy car seat, Jenna twisted up her lips in a pout. "I'm going to tell Daddy all about your presents, starting with Missy's cell phone."

Evie smiled. "I think you should, honey. I think you should tell him all about every single little detail. Maybe you could even bring Missy's cell phone with you next time y'all go visit him. That way, he'll know exactly what it was like, traveling in the car with both of you for ten hours straight."

As Jenna pondered that one, Evie popped a tape in the cassette player. "I'm going to listen to Harry Potter now. You can listen, too, or put on your headphones."

Evie pushed Play before Jenna could react. During the last few years, Evie had learned there was a time to talk, and a time to hope for silence.

As the story clicked on and cars continued to pass her minivan, Evie let her mind drift, thinking about earlier days when she'd been the one sitting in the backseat on the way to Bishop's Gate. But back then it hadn't been a minivan, it had been an early model Chevy station wagon, and she'd never minded the drive because she'd always spent the time thinking about August Meyer.

For eight summers, they'd gone from boy-girl enemies to playground buddies to true friends. They'd argued and played and flirted and finally became something more special. Each summer, they'd shared secrets and swam in the warm gulf water. Nights had been for staying up too late and laughing too much. They'd flirted just enough to make things interesting, and finally kissed the summer before her senior year.

As the scent of the ocean became more pronounced through the open sunroof, Evie grinned, knowing she had no choice but to be honest with herself. They'd done a whole lot more than just kiss. They'd discovered all about love and lust in a cove off Cascade Beach, so much so that Evie had been sure August had been the One, and that she'd been just as special to him.

But then everything changed. After one late period, she and August had pondered babies and futures and their relationship.

But when her monthly had come and with it the knowledge that no baby was on the way, the damage to their relationship had been done. Summer ended, college had come calling, and though they'd promised to stay friends, their letters and phone calls to each other became a thing of the past.

Evie had gone to Texas A&M, August to Florida State. Then she'd met John, had thought she'd found her future, and before she knew it, those summers down at Bishop's Gate at the Silver Shells Beach Resort were a distant memory.

Until her dad called on Memorial Day and said she should pack up the girls and join them for a month of fun in the sun. Evie found she couldn't say no. Life had become too hard and too stressful, the memories of happier times too vivid to ignore.

With a clunk, Missy's cell phone dropped to the floor of the backseat as she fell asleep. A quick glance in the rearview assured Evie that Jenna had done the same. Seeing that she only had fifteen miles to go, Evie dialed her mother.

"I'm on I-85, on the edge of town, Mom."

"Good! Your dad and I just got back from the store and are putting groceries away. Dad got you two six-packs of Coors Light."

Evie couldn't help but smile. Their relationship had truly come full circle. Back when she'd been a teen, she clearly recalled the night she and August had each sneaked a bottle of beer and drank them on the beach, the warm water swirling around their toes as they perched on rocks and pretended they'd never get caught.

Now her parents were buying Evie her own supply. "I'll be ready for a cold one."

"Your dad's gonna fire up the grill. You hungry?"

"I am," she said with some surprise. It had been a while since food sounded good.

"We can't wait to see the girls. Dad and I just put fresh sheets on Jenna's bed and put the crib together. You won't have to worry about a thing."

Evie could feel her shoulders relaxing. "Thanks, Mom." Evie already pictured herself in an old pair of sweats, sipping a Coors and watching the sunset, while her mother held Missy and her dad chatted with Jenna about anything and everything. She might even have ten whole minutes to sit and do nothing. Ten minutes to—

"We're going to have so much fun together, especially since the Meyers are coming over tonight."

Hold on, now. "The Meyers?"

"Yep, your dad's going out to play golf with August tomorrow morning."

"Why are they coming over tonight?"

"Because we asked them to. Goodness, Evie, it's been a full three years since you've been here. Bev said all I do is talk about Missy. She wants to see that baby."

Three years. When she and Jenna had last gone down to visit, John had been away on business, and August had been on vacation.

"Evie, is that all right?"

"Of course, Momma," she answered in a rush. "I'm

sorry, I'm just tired." And nostalgic. Gosh, seeing August again! She wasn't sure how she felt about that.

"August and Tanya are doing pretty good managing that resort. You'll have to ask them all about Silver Shores."

"I will."

"And August finally broke up with Erin, thank goodness."

Evie turned off Harry Potter and listened to her mother a little more closely. "Erin?"

"She's a local girl. I guess Erin and August knew each other back in high school. I have to tell you, Beverly and I knew from the beginning that that match wasn't meant to be."

"How long did they date?"

"Off and on a couple of years, I guess."

"I never heard about that."

Her mother paused. "Well, you were busy with John, then busy with other things."

Other things. Code for getting a divorce and trying to pick up her life. "Oh," Evie said, though that word pretty much summed up nothing.

"You're going to love catching up with August and his family, I'm sure of it," her mom said brightly. "We'll talk more when you arrive, honey. Bye!"

Stunned, Evie clicked off and pondered that one as she exited the highway, drove on the bypass, then finally took the turnoff to Silver Shells, a cottage and resort community that had been nestled in Bishop's Gate for well on twenty years.

After another series of right and left turns, she pulled into the driveway just as Jenna was waking up.

Evie had just opened her car door when her dad came trotting out.

"Hey, honey," he said, enveloping her in a hug. "Glad you made it okay."

"Me, too," she said as her dad opened the van's side panel and smiled broadly at Jenna.

"JJ!"

"Grandpa!"

Evie stood to one side as she watched her dad scoop up her eldest and shuttle her on inside, Jenna squealing in delight when he pretended to almost drop her.

As the front screen door slammed, a huge sense of relief filled Evie as she climbed in the backseat and crouched in front of Missy, whose head was listed to one side. Just looking at the sleeping twenty-two-month-old made her smile, and think every day was so worth it, even when things seemed completely insurmountable.

As she unfastened the front buckle and carefully lifted the top out from around Missy's wispy curls, her daughter's body hung limply. She had never known anyone who could sleep as soundly as Missy. Evie scooped the baby up, resting her daughter's curly-topped head against her shoulder as she backed up and began scooting out toward the door.

Only to be stopped by a hand on her hip.

"Whoa, there," the hand's owner murmured.

Whoa, was right. Though the contact had only lasted a split second, the touch vibrated through her whole body. Evie twisted out of the van, planted her feet on the ground and took a deep breath, all the while doing her best to keep Missy firmly upright.

And then it was all she could do to stand still because the man staring at her was one she would've known anywhere: August Meyer.

"Need a hand?"

She looked at his hand—big, capable, devoid of rings. And because he looked just a little bit cocky, she raised an eyebrow. "Not on my butt."

"Sorry." He didn't look the least bit contrite. "I didn't mean to scare you."

"You didn't." She juggled Missy a little closer.

His eyes softened. Green eyes that looked so familiar and warm. Comforting, like a hug. "How are you, Evie?"

Her mouth went dry as she realized she remembered far more about August than she'd ever admitted to herself. "Truthfully?"

He held up a pinkie, just like they used to do so many years ago. "Of course."

"I...I don't really know."

Chapter Two

Thankfully, August didn't have a moment to reply because her mother came flying out the front door.

"You're here! When you called and said you were close, I thought you'd maybe get here in an hour, not in fifteen minutes." Jan smiled at August before hugging Evie and scooping Missy out of her arms at the same time. Missy opened her big blue eyes and squirmed.

"I'm going to go take our baby on inside," Jan said, pressing kisses to Missy's chubby cheeks. "August, you'll help Evie unload, right?"

"It's why I'm here."

Evie blinked. His words were bland, his expression open and friendly. Their past was just that…in the past. So why did she feel as if his words held special meaning just for her?

As the screen door slammed shut again, leaving the two of them alone with just the sound of a couple of bullfrogs, August met her gaze. "It's good to see you."

"You, too. It's been a long time."

"Almost ten years."

"Yes."

He tilted his head toward the excited chatter filtering out from the cottage. "Your girls are pretty."

"Thanks. They're a handful."

"I guess all kids are."

She'd run out of words. "Maybe."

Still, he scanned her face, his green eyes looking like he was trying to memorize every feature. "I heard you got divorced."

"I did. About a year and a half ago. I heard you just had a breakup, too."

"Me and Erin weren't ever going to amount to much. It just took us a while to come to terms with it."

"It still had to be hard."

August shrugged. "If it was, it was because things didn't happen like I'd hoped. When my dad died and left me the business, Erin and I kind of fell by the wayside."

"I heard about your dad. I'm sorry."

He shrugged. "Thanks." After a moment, he gestured toward the van. "So, what can I help you with, Evie?"

There she went again, imagining a loaded question.

What *didn't* she need help with? Everything. Her life. Her job. Her complete sense of failure as a wife…running off a husband who wasn't even running to something, just away from their marriage.

But that wasn't what August had meant, and those problems weren't ones she was willing to share with him.

Instead, she pointed to the open side door. With the girls out of it, Evie thought the minivan looked a whole lot like Santa's sleigh, it was so completely packed full of toys and coolers and suitcases and baskets. "Take hold of anything you want," she said, quickly grabbing the nearest duffel and yanking it over the bucket seats.

August popped open the hatchback and pulled out two suitcases. "You never could travel light, Evie," he said with a chuckle. "Remember how you'd pack for the beach?"

She did. Her beach bag would be filled with lotions and lipstick and hair bows. Anything to make August pay attention to her.

As she followed him into the house, Evie couldn't help but notice that he still had a swimmer's body. Those shoulders were still incredibly broad, his hips lean in the worn pair of camou-colored cargo shorts. "I guess some things never change," she murmured.

The cottage was just like she remembered, except for smelling of fresh paint. Jenna was already sitting on a red-and-yellow area rug, playing with a pile of Legos her parents had dug out and watching TV. A plate of animal cookies and a glass of milk sat on a table to her right.

Evie was so relieved someone else was taking care of all the details that she didn't even care that Jenna was most likely getting too full for dinner.

August had already gone downstairs to the lower level, and Evie was about to follow when her dad stopped her and put the duffel next to the stairs. "Come have a beer, sunshine."

"The van—"

"August will get another load, and I'll help him in a minute. You need a break." Circling an arm around her shoulders, Mike led her into the bright kitchen.

After her dad thrust a cold bottle of Coors into her hand, he raised an imaginary bottle in a toast. "Cheers, dear. You made it."

"Cheers." Tears pricked at her eyes. She knew exactly what he meant. Today had certainly been a long time coming. Ever since her divorce, she'd just been subsisting, doing her best to get through each day. Weekends consisted of days alone with both girls, or days alone without them. Through it all, she still hadn't yet mastered managing her time. Agreeing to leave the state with the girls for a whole month had taken more than a leap of faith. It had been a leap without a safety net.

But John had been asked to go to Japan on business, and even he had thought it was a good time for her to get away.

As they heard the screen door screech open and slam again, duty called. "I better go help—"

Her dad held up a hand. "August, you okay?"

"I'm fine," August called back, tromping back downstairs.

Her dad grinned. "See?"

Evie leaned against the granite-topped center island. "I see. I see that you're up to something."

"Just no good." Her dad winked, the old joke they'd shared illuminating the room as brightly as the new fluorescent track lights above them.

"Momma? Momma, Missy needs to be changed, and she's hungry, too."

Ah, Jenna. The voice of reason. "I'll be right there."

"I'm taking care of it," her mother called out. "You stay in the kitchen. Mike? Come help August."

"You sit here and relax for a spell, sunshine."

Evie did, hopping up on the bar stool next to the island. She wasn't a huge drinker, but beer never tasted so good as it did at the beach. Must be something with the salty air, she supposed.

In the living room, life went on, the screen door opening and shutting, Missy fussing as her mother attempted to get that diaper changed, Jenna talking a mile a minute. The noises were comforting, familiar. Almost strange. It had been a long time since she'd sat while everyone else did the work.

After a few more minutes, August came in the kitchen with her cooler and propped it next to the stainless-steel sink. "This is the last of it."

"Thanks. I really appreciate all your help."

"It took ten minutes, Ev. No big deal."

Since she didn't want to thank him yet again, she simply nodded.

"I put the down pillow on your bed. It was yours, right?"

Now, why did that seem so personal? She swallowed. "Yes."

He stepped closer, letting her see that he, too, had grown older. Fine lines creased his eyes, the shadow of a beard graced his jaw. He was wearing cologne. Nothing too fancy, but tangy enough to set her senses on edge and make it hard to remember that she had a whole lot of other things to think about besides old memories.

"Well. I guess you're all set, then."

"I guess I am." She attempted to smile. "I swear, I'm so tired, I'm going to sleep the moment my head hits that pillow."

The doorbell rang, effectively preventing August from commenting on that. Thank God. "Mom and Tanya are here," he said, looking almost regretful. "I better go help my mom get settled."

She was just about to follow August out of the kitchen when her dad wandered in again. "Stay here and talk to me," he ordered, popping open a beer for himself and pulling out a tray of burgers, all ready for the grill. "You hungry?"

"I could be."

"I hope so. You look like hell, Evie."

"Thanks."

"You need to hear it. You're too skinny and you've got lines on your face."

"Those would be wrinkles. I am getting older, Dad."

"Not that old. More likely, I'd say you're stressed out."

Looking her over again, he shook his head. "That damn John."

Just hearing John's name could make her go from almost happy to miserable in a heartbeat. "I don't want to talk about John."

Her dad scowled, revealing his own supply of age lines. "We never have talked about him, about what he did to you. Not really."

"There was nothing to say. He didn't want to be married anymore." To her.

"He always was too selfish. The girls needed—"

"He's a good daddy." With some shock, Evie remembered how he'd never minded helping to change diapers or spend time with Jenna. How he'd been thrilled to have another girl and had visibly held back tears when Missy had been in the hospital with croup. "John's always been good to the girls."

"But never the husband you needed. He should have intended to be more than a good father—"

"Daddy, we weren't meant to be together. I've known it for a long time."

"Still, he broke your heart."

"My heart broke because I realized that my marriage had never been like I'd hoped it to be." Quietly she added, "Daddy, it wasn't like you and Momma. John and I never had a thing to say to each other at the end of the day."

Concern flickered in his gray eyes, so like her own. "But still—"

"But still, it's been hard," she agreed. Terribly hard.

After taking another sip of his beer, her dad shook his head. "Come on out to the patio and watch me cook. August's mom and sister are already out there."

"I can't wait to see Tanya. I haven't seen her since she

came out to visit last year. Do she and August stop over a lot?"

"Pretty much. August runs Silver Shells now, did you know that?"

"Yeah, I know."

"He took over when his dad had heart surgery. When Al passed, August made a lot of changes. The place was just listed in *Florida Today* as one of the top vacation resorts."

All this was news to her. "I can't believe so much has happened to August and I didn't know it."

"Why? You've had your own problems, Evie." Handing her a tray of appetizers, he said, "Let's go visit."

As they heard laughter out on the back patio, her dad's expression momentarily sobered. "It's only fair to warn you that Bev Meyer isn't doing too well."

Evie's steps faltered. "Mrs. Meyer's sick? What's wrong?"

"You'll see," he said before walking out the back door, leaving Evie to wonder what else she'd missed while unsuccessfully trying to have a life with John.

Chapter Three

Evie Ray Randall was skinny. So skinny, August figured she could put on twenty pounds and still look in need of a good meal. Her arms were too thin, her hips too bony. Dark smudges marred the translucent skin around her eyes, the shadows almost matching the smoky gray irises that had mesmerized him from the moment they'd first met.

Evie's hair needed to be cut or styled or whatever his sister, Tanya, was constantly doing to hers, because it hung down her back in a limp ponytail, the once vibrant color dull and faded.

So, how come he still thought Evie was the most beautiful woman in the world?

It had to be the spark of mischief that never quite left her eyes. The way she was never too sweet, too patient, or too upbeat. In short, Evie Ray had always been *real*. She laughed when things were funny, showed her temper when she was mad, and cried at Hallmark commercials. Yep, with Evie, what you saw was what you got. And he'd always wanted every bit of her.

"What?" Evie asked, catching him staring from across the table they were setting. "Do I have ketchup on me or something?" She picked up a napkin she'd just folded and swiped it across her face.

"Stop, you look fine," he said, grabbing the napkin. "I didn't mean to stare, I was just thinking of something else."

She pulled a stack of plates from the basket her mom had set out and started walking around the table, placing each in the center of a red linen place mat. "Really? It must have been pretty important."

When he took too long formulating a reply, she gestured toward the far side of the patio. "Are you worried about your mom?"

"No. Well, not too much." Out of habit, he studied his mom's color as she munched on a bacon-wrapped shrimp. For the moment, his mother looked healthy, her color not too flushed.

Evie leaned forward. "My dad told me that she's been sick."

"Yeah. She's had some trouble with her cholesterol and blood pressure, among other things. She had to have a stent put in one of her arteries last year. Unfortunately, I don't think it's slowed her down for a minute."

"What gave you the first clue?" Evie asked with a broad grin. "The pile of shrimp or the plate of fries my dad just handed her?"

"All of it," he said, finally able to see the humor. Bev Meyer had never been one to follow anyone's advice but her own. Why had he thought things would suddenly change? "I'm trying to take care of her, but she wants none of it."

"She's always been independent."

Thinking of his mother, who'd once been a ballet teacher before settling down to raise kids and help her husband with the resort, he nodded. "Yeah. She has always been that."

"Things have been tough since your dad died, huh?" she asked, handing him the spoons as she folded napkins and began circling the table once again.

Dutifully, August placed a spoon to the right of each

plate. "Yep, but at least Tanya lives nearby, too. She moved next to Mom, just in case Mom starts feeling bad but doesn't want to tell us. The first time Tanya and I heard Mom was having heart problems was when her doctor told us they'd admitted her to the hospital."

"Oh, August."

He tried to smile, to ease Evie's look of worry. "It sucked. Luckily, she's promised she'll never keep us in the dark again."

"She better not."

Determined to lighten the mood, he pointed to the chunky blue salt-and-pepper shakers on the table. "These look familiar. They're from your catalog, right?"

"Yep. Mom and Dad are great customers."

"I looked through it the other day. You do a great job."

"It's not *my* catalog. I just work there and help manage things. It's a good place to work."

"It's great they let you take a long vacation."

"Summer is a slow time for us." With a shrug, she added, "Plus, I needed a break."

"Being here in Bishop's Gate will be good for you."

Emotion sparked in her eyes. "Lately, I've been hearing that a lot. I must look even worse than I thought." Before he could say a word, Evie pointed to the flight of steps leading out toward the walkway and beach. "The table's all set. Let's go sit out there."

"All right." Grabbing two more Coors Lights, August told everyone they were going for a short walk, then followed Evie, who'd already stepped off the patio, kicked off her shoes, and was walking barefoot down the path.

In a couple of strides, he caught up with her. "I got us another round."

"Thanks," she said, twisting off the cap easily.

After a few more steps, they sat down on a pair of

ancient iron chairs, half buried in silky-soft warm sand. Within seconds, Evie buried her toes in the sand, too. "Ah," she said, finally treating him to a genuine smile. "Do you smell the surf? I love it here."

August stretched out his legs and glanced toward the horizon, where the warm gulf water rushed in gentle waves across the shoreline. "Me, too. I've always loved it here." Beside him, Evie sat with her head back, sheer bliss on her face. She looked beautiful. "For the record, I think you look okay, Evie," he said softly.

Her head popped up, her eyes so full of cautious eagerness, that it took his breath away. "Yeah?"

"Yeah," he replied, hoping she didn't hear how affected by her he was. He took a fortifying sip of his Coors and watched the waves with Evie.

Little by little, the sunlight faded and the temperature dropped. Behind them, August could hear his mom laugh at some old joke Mike was telling.

"You just need to take some time for yourself," he added after a while.

She laughed at that. "What I need to do, August, is take care of my children."

August pointed behind them. On the patio, Missy was playing with some French fries on the tray of her high chair and Jenna was showing Tanya her collection of naked Barbie dolls. "Your girls look fine."

Her expression softened. "Right now, at this minute, I guess they do."

Her pleasure in his simple compliment brought back all kinds of memories for August. "Remember when we went to that carnival and got stuck on the Ferris wheel?"

She chuckled. "Don't act like that was a rare occurrence. I think everyone in Bishop's Gate has gotten stuck on that Ferris wheel one time or another."

"I won't deny that. Still—do you remember the night it was our turn?"

"Absolutely. I remember that it was pretty much the hottest night of the year."

It *had* been hot. Evie had worn short jean shorts, blistering white Keds and a bright teal halter top. She'd been all smooth, tan skin and golden hair. Gorgeous. "You were the only girl who didn't panic when the wind picked up and our seat started rocking."

Evie leaned closer, her bare arm brushing against his…just like they had so long ago. "That's because I was the only girl who had August Anderson Meyer's arm around her."

He remembered that well. Her skin had felt like satin, and there'd been enough humor in her eyes to make being stuck on the ancient ride a true adventure.

He'd kissed her, too. He'd pulled her so close that their seat had rocked quite a bit, all on its own. "That was a great night, though your parents never did push back curfew."

Evie smiled. "They weren't fools—they knew what we wanted to do. Jenna's got another thing coming if she thinks she'll ever pull one over on me."

Back on the porch, Jenna was showing Jan a picture she'd just colored. "It's for Daddy," she pronounced, her voice floating toward them.

Evie visibly winced as she stared at the water once again.

"You okay?"

"Oh, sure. I'm, uh, having a tough time remembering not to care that I took the girls away from their dad—from John—for a whole month."

"Did John not want you to come to Florida?"

She looked surprised. "He encouraged me, actually.

He's going to be gone most of the month, and he knows just how much the girls love my parents."

"So, you and your ex still get along."

"Well enough. He's there for the girls whenever he can be." Digging her toes deeper into the sand, she added, "John's always been a good father. A very good father."

Her defense of the guy made August seethe. She was hurting. He saw it now, and he'd heard about it from her parents. She looked worn-out and stressed, overworked and underfed. August knew her ex-husband was the reason...so why was she defending the guy? "A good father...but not a good husband?"

Gray eyes widened and a hint of a smile played around the corners of her pale pink lips. "I don't know about that. I think he just fell out of love."

"Did you?"

"I don't know. Honestly, some days...some nights I wonder if I'd ever really been in love with him." She shook her head. "I was on cruise control, you know? I went to work, I came home, I cooked dinner. On my days off I vacuumed and cleaned the house. Sometimes I remembered to wear makeup." Quietly, she added, "Sometimes I remembered to give John my attention. Sometimes he remembered, too."

August hated the thought of her so unhappy. "He should have helped you more."

"It wasn't me, it wasn't him...it was 'us.' And 'us' wasn't good. We made babies. We raised them together. We divided chores and shared a checkbook, but I don't know if we ever shared a life."

It sounded like a cop-out to August. "I can't believe he left you and the girls."

"He didn't, not really. He's nearby, he helps. He just left *me*."

He hated that she so obviously thought it was her fault. August clasped her hand, unable to keep from touching her. "Evie—"

She squeezed his hand to stop his words. "At first I was devastated. But then one night when I was all alone, sipping wine and feeling sorry for myself, I remembered our honeymoon. There we were, sporting shiny gold rings. We'd just had the most amazing wedding and reception, were finally free to do whatever we wanted, whenever we wanted—and I didn't have a thing to say to him."

Stark awareness filled her eyes as she met his gaze. "And that's when I *knew,* August. Three months after our divorce, as I sat on my couch, remembering a thousand little details, I knew John had been right. We'd jumped into marriage and into grown-up life without ever jumping into love. And, as much as it pains me to admit it…that wasn't enough. John and I, we had no passion."

No passion.

The details of her life were hard to hear, though August had wanted to hear every bit. Back in high school, he'd had a major crush on Evie Ray. The last summer when they were together, when they thought she was pregnant, he'd fantasized about a future with her in it. When their "scare" was over, he'd been almost disappointed. Enough to think about persuading her to not go back to Texas, to attend Florida State with him.

But something had vanished between them. Once more, he'd been too unsure of himself to try and make things better. He'd felt that regret time and again through the years.

He should have done more to make her see he was worth it. That *they* were worth it.

"If John fell out of love, the problem was his, not yours," he murmured, running his thumb over her knuckles.

"I guess." Evie said the words almost wistfully, almost as if she didn't believe him, which made August wonder just how much she'd begun to doubt herself. Did she not feel she deserved anything?

"Momma? Momma, I can't find Neena," Jenna announced from the patio, loud enough for everyone on the beach to know that she had a problem.

Evie dropped August's hand like it was on fire and got to her feet just as Jenna darted down the steps to them. "Neena is Jenna's baby doll," Evie explained. "Any chance you saw it when you were unloading?"

August shook his head, not failing to notice the switch in her posture, the change in her voice. "I don't remember a doll, but I don't think I looked under the seats, either. Maybe it's still there?"

"Maybe."

Jenna slipped in between them. "Momma, what about Neena?"

With a wry expression, Evie ruffled her daughter's curls. "Let's go look in the van, sugar." Without looking back, Evie slipped on her sandals and guided Jenna back to the house.

August picked up the half-full bottle of beer Evie had abandoned and followed, too, feeling curiously left behind as the girl jabbered and complained and Evie nodded sympathetically.

When they reached the patio, Jenna's voice turned whiny. "I'm tired, Momma. I want Neena."

Evie gave her a quick hug. "I know you are. We'll find Neena then get ready for bed." Almost as an afterthought, Evie turned to August. "See you," she whispered. "I've got to go."

"Wait a minute." He pointed to the table they'd just set. "Aren't you going to eat?"

"I will—later."

Frustration coursed through August, tempting him to take charge. He wanted to tell Jenna to wait a minute and let her mother eat. To tell her parents to go look for the doll instead of watching Evie do it.

But it wasn't his place.

As Jenna started crying in earnest, Evie picked her up and headed to the front of the house where her van was parked. Catching his eye, she smiled. "Don't worry, August."

But August knew he would. In many ways, he'd never stopped worrying about Evie. Not when he thought he'd gotten her pregnant.

Not when she'd called to say that everything was fine and no baby was in the future.

Not even when he'd come to the conclusion that maybe what they'd felt hadn't been love—just more like teenage hormones on overdrive.

There'd always been a part of August that would worry about Evie Ray. He wasn't about to stop now.

Chapter Four

The baby doll had been found. Dinner had been consumed, the golf game between August and Mike confirmed, and after promises to get together soon, the Meyer family had taken off.

After a bout of too-tired tears, Evie had gotten the girls bathed, unpacked and asleep. She then padded into her own room, decorated in soft blues and grays, as soothing as a hot bubble bath in the middle of January. Her mother had placed a vanilla candle on the whitewashed dresser, and stuck six spunky daisies in a tall, thin glass.

The tiny bedroom felt cozy and comfortable and more like home than her bedroom suite in her old house in Grapevine.

Undoubtedly, her parents were upstairs, probably waiting for her to reappear so they could have a nice chat, but honestly, Evie wasn't up for it. The silence was too sweet, the crisp cotton sheets too beckoning.

She sank on the lace coverlet with a sigh and finally relaxed. She'd done it. She'd made it to Florida, and she'd made it through a first conversation with August, which had been an odd mix of tenderness and crazy swirling emotions.

Yawning, Evie stretched back against the padded headboard.

Seeing August had been something of a shock to her system. She'd firmly put him in the back of her mind, in the shadows of her past. She'd had no desire to think about what could have been. No reason to remember what almost was.

Being in the same room with him had opened a million senses, and made everything in her body feel electrified. His touch had made her warm. His caring looks made her pulse race erratically. During that whole conversation with him, Evie'd noticed her brain fogging up, encouraging her to reveal things about her marriage to John that she never shared with anyone…and making that little voice in her heart wonder if maybe she wasn't as shut down and worn-out as she'd previously thought.

Evie curled onto her side, hugging the down pillow August had placed on her bed, and tried not to feel so much.

"Evie, you okay?" After a brief knock, her mom popped her head in. "Dad and I were wondering if you were going to come back up and visit a while."

Hastily, Evie released the pillow and sat up. "Sorry. I think the trip has caught up with me. I think I'm going to go to sleep."

"Oh. Well, all right." Her mom pattered on in, ignoring the subtle hint and invading her space, just like she always had. "I'm sure you remember where everything is. There's more blankets in the hall closet. More pillows, too."

Evie patted the one from home. The one with the pretty yellow case August had placed neatly in the center of the bed. "I'll be fine. I think that second beer I had with August was a mistake."

"Probably not the talk, though. You two looked like you were picking up where you left off."

"I don't know about that." But it had been nice to visit with him. Nicer than she would have ever imagined. And because she felt ridiculous even thinking his touching her pillow was worth a second thought, Evie kept her voice level. "He's a good guy."

Jan sat down next to Evie, a puff of White Linen perfume floating around her, mixing with the sheets... making everything smell comfortable and familiar. "That August, he's so considerate."

He'd been more than that. He'd listened to her and made her feel more relaxed than she had in an entire year. "He was really helpful, unpacking the van and all."

Jan picked up a pillow that had fallen on the floor and neatly set it against the headboard. "You two sure looked like you were having quite a conversation."

"Just catching up."

Her mom nodded. "You've got years of that to do. Maybe you should spend some time together."

The words were spoken casually. So casually that Evie knew that her mother was up to no good. Drawing from past experience, Evie nipped her matchmaking in the bud. "I'm not here for another summer romance, Mom. I'm here to see you and Dad and have fun with the girls."

"I know, but if something came along, that might be nice, don't you think?"

No, she did not. Evie couldn't even imagine having time or energy for a relationship. As it was now, she was lucky if she remembered to eat. "I'm really tired."

For a split second, her mom scanned her face. Emotion filled her gaze, so strong it brought back memories of major events in their lives...Evie's graduation, Jenna's birth. Evie's announcement that she and John had separated. With a sigh, Jan stood up. "All righty. See you in the morning. Good night, Evelyn."

Evelyn said, "'Night, Mom."

Alone again, Evie opened her suitcase, pulled out two cosmetic bags and got ready for bed. She had just crawled under the thick down comforter when she realized she'd forgotten to call John to let him know that they got there safe and sound.

Quickly, she dialed his number on her cell phone, and got his voice mail, as expected. "It's me. We got to Florida, no problem. The girls say 'Hey.' Jenna's already drawn you two pictures. I'll pop them in the mail soon." Then, remembering how much John hated the fancy dinners he always had to attend on his business trips, she added, "I hope you remembered to pack some peanut butter. 'Bye."

With that, she turned off the light and pulled the sheets up to her chin. As she closed her eyes, so many thoughts filled her mind. Her past, her present.

The lack of dreams about a future, except for the ones that focused solely on the girls.

And, strangely, her mother's sunny optimism for romance.

"MOMMA, GRANDMA SAYS I gotta eat egg sandwiches," Jenna announced from the foot of Evie's bed the next morning. "I hate eggs."

Evie opened one eye to see just how upset her daughter was. A pouty lip meant not too much. Blotchy cheeks meant a real crisis was at hand and tears were on the way.

Jenna was holding Neena for dear life and balancing a tilting egg-sandwich-laden plate in the other. As Evie expected, Jenna's cheeks were red enough to make another woman think she needed sunscreen. *Uh-oh.*

"Oh, Jen." Evie rolled over and held out her arms. "Put the plate down and come give me a hug."

Jenna put down the plate and scooted forward, pink puppy dog pajamas riding up her calves as she slipped under the covers.

Evie cuddled her close, loving the coconut shampoo scent in her daughter's hair and the faint fragrance of hot chocolate surrounding her. When Jenna visibly relaxed, Evie said, "Now, what's going on?"

Big gray eyes, full of worry and belligerence, stared back at her. "Grandma doesn't want me just eating Cheerios. She said I get eggs."

"And you said—"

"I don't like eggs. I hate eggs! But she didn't listen." Jenna shifted to glare at the egg sandwich on the floor. "That's when she handed me that."

Evie sat up, eyeing the plate. *Ugh.* She'd always hated eggs, too. "And that's when you decided to get some help."

"Yep. I won't eat it, Momma. I won't."

"You don't have to."

"Really?"

"Really. I know you don't like eggs. I don't like them, either. Cheerios are fine. What's Missy doing?"

"Playing with Grandpa, but he says he can't stay much longer cause he's gonna go play golf."

"Boy, I better get up." Glancing at the clock, Evie did a double take. Nine! When was the last time she'd slept so late?

Jenna pulled back the covers and hopped out, Evie following more slowly. "I hope Grandma made coffee," she muttered under her breath.

"I hope Grandma made me cereal," Jenna said with the exact same intonation as she led the way upstairs.

Evie threw on a robe, picked up the offending plate and followed. Sure enough, her mother was at the stove, making still more egg sandwiches. "Hey, Mom."

"Jenna shouldn't have woken you up." Looking around, Jan said, "Where's your plate, young lady?"

Jenna scooted onto the chair. "Momma said I can have Cheerios."

Jan put her spatula down and pivoted to the kitchen table. "Jenna, you watch your mouth. Evie, tell her—"

"Mom, Jenna won't eat eggs. I thought you knew that."

"But—"

"She won't. Ever. Let her have some cereal and a banana. It's good for her."

"What about you?"

"I'll eat something, soon," Evie said, getting a mug and pouring a generous amount of coffee and cream into it.

With a flick of her wrist, Evie watched her mother turn off the burner and pull out a giant box of Cheerios. "Feed your daughter," she said, thrusting the box at her with a sharp look. "Then feed yourself something. Anything."

"Oh, Jan. Leave Evie and Jenna alone," her dad said as he rose from the couch. "Nothing wrong with Cheerios."

"Morning, Daddy."

"Morning, sunshine," Mike said, propping Missy on his hip and taking a seat across from Jenna. "How'd you sleep?"

Evie leaned close and kissed Missy on the forehead. "Great."

A knock sounded at the door, then it opened slowly, revealing August in a faded blue golf shirt, khaki shorts and a worn leather belt. "Hello?"

Mike smiled brightly. "Hey, August, come on in. Want something to eat?"

August eyed the kitchen counter. "Got any egg sandwiches?"

Mike winked at Evie. "You bet. Jan, can you make August some breakfast?"

As they all expected, Jan bustled back in and hurried to get August a plate. Mike laughed.

Finally, August turned to her. "How are you this morning, Evie?"

She'd just rolled out of bed. She'd barely had a cup of coffee. Her daughter was pouty and her mother was ticked at her. "I'm…good. You?"

"Me?" August looked her over, for some reason making her feel pretty and attractive instead of in need of a hot shower…and well, a makeover. A slow smile lit his eyes. "I'm perfect," he drawled.

For a split second, Evie felt perfect, too.

Chapter Five

"Watch your toes!" Evie cried to Missy as the toddler pulled herself up onto a big rock and scrunched her tiny toes in the powder-soft sand next to Evie's towel and umbrella on the edge of Cascade Beach. "The sand's hot!"

"Hop," Missy mumbled, squishing her toes again in the sand before plopping down on her bottom.

Evie rolled to one side and watched her baby girl giggle as she scooped up a handful of sand and looked at it in her palm before letting it flow through her fingers. "Oh, Missy. You bring me joy."

"She'd bring anyone joy," Tanya said from her left. "Missy is such a sweetheart."

Evie couldn't deny it. From the moment Missy had been born, she was Jenna's polar opposite. Easygoing, sleepy at night, happy with life. Evie could only imagine what life would have been like with two Jennas. Most likely, she'd have white hair and be talking with a stutter. "I'm lucky."

"You are that. You have two adorable girls while I'm still trying to find Mr. Right."

Thinking about John, Evie now knew there was a whole lot more to people than labels. "'Mr. Right' isn't as easy to find as you might think. Actually, 'Mr. Right' might not even exist."

Tanya's shoulders slumped. "I suppose not. But, still…"

"But still…I know." Evie knew what Tanya meant. It would be nice to find someone who was as good as his first impression. Someone who lived up to expectations.

As Tanya stretched out her legs on the beach towel, she smiled at Missy and her handful of sand. "She's so adorable, she makes me want to have a baby."

"Be careful what you wish for. Missy's a good girl, but she had me up for almost two days straight when she was getting her front teeth. You may like sleeping."

"I hadn't thought about that."

"I have a feeling there's a lot about raising a kid that you might not have thought about," Evie said with a smile.

"Maybe so." Tanya chuckled. "I do like eating adult food…not things with cartoons on their containers." As she picked up a bag of fruit snacks, she shook her head. "I can't believe you eat these."

"I don't, Jenna does." Well, Evie had been known to eat through a whole box when there was nothing else in the house. "And speaking of Jenna, I hope she's not driving my mom batty at the grocery store."

Tanya winked. "I bet she's only asking for one thing in each aisle."

"You do know my daughter."

"I learned a thing or two from my visits to Texas over the years."

Tanya had visited her and John at least one weekend a year from the time they'd both graduated college. Every time, their friendship had seemed to pick up exactly where it had left off. Consequently, Tanya had been the only person who hadn't been surprised when Evie announced her separation.

Laughing, Evie said, "If my mom only has to deal with food requests, she's getting off pretty easily."

Still rummaging in the beach bag, Tanya pulled out a box of Goldfish. "Now these, I like."

"You'd look at them as a gourmet treat in no time," Evie commented. "You'd have a good feeling about juice boxes, too."

"I would if I could add a shot of vodka on occasion. Hey, speaking of drinks, we're probably due for something cold and wet, too." Tanya popped open the cooler she'd brought from home. "I've got Diet Coke or iced tea. Which one?"

"Sweet tea?"

Tanya looked properly horrified. "Is there any other?"

Evie smiled at their old joke. "Tea, then, please."

Tanya unscrewed the top of a large glass jar, poured out two cupfuls, added some ice out of a plastic baggie, and handed the cup to Evie, who smiled appreciatively. "You are a sweet tea genius."

In a ridiculous Elvis impersonation, Tanya bowed. "Thank you, thank you very much." After closing the cooler, Tanya sat down next to Evie. "So, you've been here two days. Are you relaxing yet?"

"Getting there. My body's going through shock, I think, from getting so much rest and relaxation." Not wanting to discuss her health with one more person, she sipped her tea and turned the tables. "What's new with you?"

After handing Missy a juice box, Tanya shrugged. "Not much. I've moved next to my mother and teach ballet at her old studio."

"Do you like that? You always had dreams of going to New York."

Tanya smiled. "I think every dancer has that dream. To answer your question, I do like it, but I don't love it. I'm not the teacher my mother was."

"You might be."

"I'm not. My mother was a born instructor—I wanted to perform. The two are pretty different entities." Curving her legs underneath her, Tanya said, "I'm having to learn a lot about patience."

The confession made Evie realize that they'd all given up some dreams at one time or another. Obviously, that was what growing up was all about—picking and choosing the path to take. "August told me you're helping him, too."

"I am…well, I work at the resort as much as August asks me to."

"Asks you? What's up with that? The Tanya I know takes what she wants when she wants it."

"We both know I haven't been that demanding in years. Besides, I've been trying to give August some space. He's still trying to get over his breakup with Erin and, well, he feels a lot of responsibility for Silver Shells. It makes him grumpy at times."

Erin. For a second, Evie thought about asking about August and Erin, but decided against it. She focused on the easier subject instead. "Grumpy, that's hard for me to imagine."

"Oh, he's not mean, August just likes things how he likes them, and forgets to ask for help. But with Silver Shells doing such good business, he can use all the help he can get. Especially with Mom. She can be trying at times."

Remembering August's frequent glances at his mom while they were setting the table, Evie nodded. "August seems worried."

"He is. We both are. Neither of us wants to see her go through some of the procedures my dad was subjected to."

Thinking of Beverly's robust laugh at the barbecue, Evie said, "I thought she looked great."

"She does. All those years of ballet have helped her bones. But her cholesterol's off the charts. She's ornery, too." Tanya shrugged. "I don't want to bore you, but taking care of someone who doesn't want to be taken care of gets tiring, especially now that I've moved next to her. Sometimes I just want to tell her to remember her age."

That sounded like trouble. "Maybe she'll settle down soon."

Tanya laughed and stretched out her legs, flexing her poor, calloused toes. "Maybe she will. And maybe one day the perfect man will appear out of the surf and take me away."

After righting Missy's lopsided juice box, Evie scanned the horizon. "I'll be on the lookout."

"Believe me, he hasn't had the nerve to come around yet. I'm kind of ornery myself." After a moment, Tanya said, "I'm kind of surprised you aren't."

"What's that supposed to mean?"

"After everything you've been through, you don't seem bitter or angry."

"That's because I'm not. Just tired," Evie replied, telling the truth. All she wanted to do was sleep and sit on the beach and watch the tide come in and out.

"Luckily, you have someone lying in wait."

Evie glanced at the horizon again. "You're completely confused, T."

"Stop. You know who I'm talking about." Tanya batted her eyes at Evie. "I mean my brother would love to be your knight in shining armor, and I bet you might just let him be that again."

"Again?" As close as they were, August was the one subject Evie never discussed with her friend. Just how much did Tanya know about their past?

"Yes, again."

For a split second, Evie recalled their frantic phone calls when her period had been late and his vows that he'd take care of her.

The sinking feeling she'd had, not wanting to be taken care of. The relief when she'd called him and told him that everything was fine and there would be no need to plan futures again…or, at least not for four more years.

"There's something, Evie. August doesn't just pop over to your parents' house for breakfast any day of the week."

Evie bit back a wave of irritation. Suddenly everyone around her was expecting she and August to take up from where they'd left off. "I don't know why August came over."

Tanya kept talking. "There always was something special between the two of you. Could be again."

"No chance. I can hardly take care of myself and the girls. I couldn't take care of a boyfriend, too."

"I don't think August is going to want to be taken care of. Probably the opposite. If I know him, he's going to want to take care of you."

"Then that worries me, too. I never want to feel obligated to a man ever again."

Tanya curved her arms around her bent knees. "Maybe you should, just a little. I always thought you were a little too standoffish around John."

Evie stiffened. "I don't know what you're talking about." She kept her gaze on Missy, who was using a beach chair to pull herself up.

"Sure, you do. Remember when I came out to visit when Jenna was two and you had a cold?"

Evie remembered. John had wanted her to go to the doctor and get a strep test. She'd pretty much told him to mind his own business. Tanya had had trouble keeping her mouth shut.

"I don't want anyone taking care of me. Besides, August lives here and I'm in Texas. Getting involved in a long-distance relationship would be a pretty dumb move on my part, if I was looking to get into a relationship." Which she wasn't.

"I suppose."

Suddenly, Missy tumbled and fell, taking in a mouthful of sand. Spitting and crying, she rubbed her mouth and eyes, which of course got more sand and salt in them. Then the wailing began.

Hastily, Evie wiped down the baby's face while Tanya searched through the humongous straw tote for baby wipes. Still Missy cried on.

"Uh-oh," Tanya said, her face filled with panic. "What does she need?"

"To get cleaned off," Evie said around Missy's crying body, which had attached itself to her chest and neck like a giant starfish. "Get me some bottled water, please."

"Oh. Yeah."

After Evie got a bottle of Aquafina and practically drenched Missy's face, the tears finally started to subside.

When she was sure she'd gotten all the sand out of Missy's eyes she held her daughter close and murmured, "Poor Missy. I'm so sorry that happened."

Missy's thumb popped in her mouth in record time, her eyes slowly drifting shut. Now that the mini-crisis was over, Evie leaned back against the canvas chair, breathing a sigh of relief. "I think we're all better now."

"Barely all better. That scared the life out of me. I think I need a drink." Tanya opened her cooler again, so quickly that Evie couldn't figure out if she was teasing or not. "Maybe I have some beer in here."

"It's eleven in the morning! You don't need a drink, you just need to breathe deep."

"Breathing's not working."

"It will. This wasn't a disaster." Evie couldn't hide the amusement in her voice. If Tanya could have seen her and the girls when she'd slit her hand open slicing a tomato and both girls in hysterics at the sight of all the blood, she'd know what a real state of emergency was.

"I can't believe you were so calm," Tanya continued. "I was freaking out."

"That's because you don't have any kids."

"Now I know why. I'm taking back everything I said about wanting a baby."

Though Missy was now sleeping soundly, Evie wasn't in a hurry to set her down. Instead, she shifted Missy and made sure she was protected by the umbrella's shade before relaxing. "You'll get used to it."

"I suppose."

Though outwardly calm, inside Evie could privately admit to being a little shaken up, too. For a moment, she hadn't been able to remember where the bottled water and clean towels were and had been frustrated when Tanya simply stared at her instead of acting quickly.

Closing her eyes, she rolled her head and tried to loosen the knot that had formed along the base of her neck. Tried to pretend that she didn't mind all the responsibility. Tried to relax. Once again, it was easier said than done.

Chapter Six

August was on the phone with his accountant, but all he could think about was Evie.

He'd started a list of activities to entertain her and her two girls. And before he deluded himself into thinking it was for old time's sake, he admitted the plain and simple truth: he wanted to be near her.

In fact, there was no way he was going to be within a mile of Evie Ray and not do his best to be in her presence. There was still a spark between them that had him thinking about pulling her into the shadows and kissing her.

Looking at his calendar, August saw that she'd already been there a full week and he'd only seen her a few times. Though his schedule looked busy, there was nothing on it that couldn't be changed for more fun activities.

Maybe Evie would want to take the girls to the putt-putt course.

"August, need anything else?"

August couldn't recall the last five things his accountant had told him. "Nope. I'll be in touch if I think of something we forgot to discuss. Thanks for the phone call, Steve," he said before disconnecting the call as fast as he could.

When blessed silence surrounded him, he stared at his notes again. Maybe he'd ask Evie if she wanted to go on a cruise around the bay with the girls.

"August? August, you busy?"

He looked up to see his mom hovering outside his door. He stood. "What's up, Mom?"

"My bridge game was over early. Pat Kampf is sick."

August couldn't even remember all of his mother's friends who were in poor health. "How are you feeling?"

"Good." She waved a hand. "I have some business to discuss."

"Okay." Slowly he sat back down as his mom crossed to one of the chairs in front of his desk. "Do you need something?"

"Money."

This was unchartered territory. His mom had her own accounts, but had invested the bulk of her money in August's name in case something happened to her. August had agreed to the arrangement reluctantly…only with the knowledge that his mother could have free and easy access to the funds whenever she wanted.

But this was the first time in two years that she'd ever asked. "Okay." He got out his checkbook. "How much do you need?"

To his surprise, she looked taken aback. "You're not going to grill me?"

"You're my mother. Of course I'm not going to ask you questions about why you need money. Besides, we both agreed you were in charge of your own funds, right?"

"Right. But this might be different." She hedged. "It's a lot."

August tried to keep his voice light, though inside he was really curious. What the devil was going on? "I assumed it was, since you saw the need to ask me and all."

"This is hard. I don't know how you're going to react."

Absently twirling the pen in between his fingers, he looked his mother over a little more carefully. Now he was getting worried. Was she sick? "How much do you need, Mom?"

"Three thousand dollars."

He dropped his pen. Warily, he raised his head. His mother was sitting there across from him, rigid and tense, obviously begging for a fight.

He was frightened enough to let her have one. Was her insurance not paying for her drugs the way they'd planned on? "What happened? Are you sick?"

She rolled her eyes. "Honestly, August. I'm fine. This money is for…personal reasons."

Huh? "Mom—"

"You said you wouldn't interfere."

"That's before I knew you wanted three thousand dollars." And before she was acting so strange.

She bit her lip. "It's not for me. Not, really."

"What is it for?"

"A club."

"What kind of club?"

"A social one. August, there's no other way to tell you this but straight out." She took a deep breath and plunged in, saying the words in a jumbled mess. "For your information, I'm joining Harmonious Haven."

Harmonious Haven. The singles club advertised during late-night syndicated shows on Channel 12. Couple after couple were highlighted, each looking more fit, handsome and romantic than the last. The couples made the match-making Internet site sound like the best thing since sliced bread, but August knew it had to be a scam.

Falling in love was never that easy.

Before he could think twice, all of August's good intentions about being supportive of his mother went out the window. "Mom—"

"Don't you 'Mom' me. I know what I'm doing."

"It doesn't sound like it." Before he thought better of it, he said, "What happened to Dad?"

"Your father is buried at Park Hill, thank you very much."

August blinked, amazed at just how much her words could hurt. "He's barely been gone a year."

"He was sick for a long time before that."

"And your point is?"

His mother jabbed one French-manicured finger toward him. "Watch your mouth."

"Watch my mouth? You watch yourself."

"I need companionship."

Companionship? Was she talking about sex? For a split second, he recalled the last time he and Erin had gone to bed. When had that been? Two months ago? Three?

It felt like a hell of a long time. "It's not my business if you want to join Harmonious Haven," he said slowly, doing his best to try and forget about his own lack of love life and focus on his mother's. "I just think this is coming from out of the blue."

"For you, maybe. For me, I've been thinking about joining for a while. I've been surfing the Web site."

"Surfing?" When had she gotten so computer-savvy?

She continued as though he'd never spoken. "I even called the number and asked some questions. HH is a member of the Better Business Bureau."

Now that he thought about it, his mother looked…fresh. Like she'd gone somewhere besides Suzy's Salon to get her hair done. Like she'd gone to one of those fancy counters at the mall and gotten her makeup refreshed. Like she got one of those BOTOX injections and was looking better for it.

It all made him a little squeamish. "You've got a heart condition."

"But it's still beating, August."

"But—"

"I'm better, August," she said more gently. "The doctors say I'm better. I feel better. I'm ready to do things again. That's why I need to join now."

Somewhere in the back of his mind, August realized just how hard it must have been for his mom to have to come to him for money. And to tell him the truth. After all, she certainly didn't owe him any explanations.

Picking up the pen again, he said, "Is three thousand enough?"

"It's enough."

August pretended he didn't notice that her eyes were shining. That she looked…happy. Signing the check, he handed it to her. "Will you be mad if I asked you to be careful?"

Her eyes softened and she stood, giving him a quick kiss on the cheek. "I'd be sad if you didn't care. Thank you, dear."

When he was alone again, August picked up the phone and started dialing Evie's phone number. Obviously it was time to take some risks.

Chapter Seven

Jenna looked her mother up and down, paused to consider the invitation, then very carefully shook her head. "I don't wanna go."

It was a losing battle, but Evie braced herself to try again. She wanted to go on the cruise with August, but she could admit that she was chicken enough to need reinforcements. "Jenna, if you don't go, you'll wish you did."

Jenna gave her a look that suggested she seriously doubted that. "What about Missy?"

"Missy's too little to go on a boat, you know that."

Hugging Neena tightly, Jenna scooted closer to the television remote. "I don't wanna go, Momma. Me and Neena like staying here."

"All right." In spite of herself, Evie couldn't help but admire her eldest daughter's steadfastness. Actually, Evie wished she could borrow a little of that quality for herself. Ever since her phone conversation that morning with August, she'd gone through the gamut of emotions. Surprise that August asked her out, happiness that she could still get a date. Then, of course, pure fright set in.

Evie didn't know how to date anymore. In her mind, dating was what she'd done in college. Those dates had involved bars and clubs, fraternity parties and walks on campus. It was fast-food restaurants and cheap movies.

She was pretty sure August knew how to date. She was fairly sure there was some dating ritual all current singles employed. They knew whether to open their car door or not. Whether to buy drinks or wait to be served. Knew the classy, happening clubs, listened to bands that didn't cater to toddlers and wore the right shoes.

All Evie had been into lately was strawberry Quik, Kids Bop and a sturdy pair of Clarks.

Even though the battle was over and Jenna had come out victorious, Evie tried one last time. "I bet we'll see lots of pretty fish."

"Grandma's taking me to the aquarium tomorrow," her daughter volleyed right back. "Remember?" There was that tone again, the one her daughter had mastered mere months after learning to talk. Authoritative. Sure. Border-line bossy.

Desperation set in. If she didn't have Jenna as a buffer, Evie was going to have to deal with this cruise as an actual date. Even though she knew it was a lost cause, she started thinking bribery might be in order. "What if—"

"Evie, honey, stop."

In unison, Evie and her daughter turned to Jan in surprise.

"I didn't see you there," Evie mumbled.

"Obviously not." Pointing to the kitchen table, her mother said, "Come sit down for a second, dear."

As obediently as when she was ten, Evie crossed the living room and sat down at the kitchen table next to her mom. Jenna watched her with a glint of satisfaction, then clicked on the remote, smiled when she saw *Dora the Explorer* was on and went back to playing with Neena.

After opening the Tupperware cabinet for Missy, Jan pressed her hands on her thighs. "Here's the deal, Ev.

Jenna and Missy don't want to go sit on a boat. I can't say I blame them, either. Boats and children really don't mix. They're going to want to get off after twenty minutes and that won't be an option."

"Jenna might really enjoy it."

Her mother laughed. "Jenna might really enjoy having pizza for dinner. She might really enjoy making a new dress for her doll. She will not enjoy a cruise." Leveling a look at Evie, Jan said softly, "You know I'm right."

She knew. Her mother was absolutely right. But that didn't mean she had to give in gracefully. "Maybe."

"You're a good mother, and therefore you know what I mean when I tell you that all good mothers need to pick their battles. You could force your eldest to go, but I think you'd regret it. Jenna in a power play isn't pretty."

No. No, she wasn't. Jenna in full battle mode was pretty much a remake of *The War of the Worlds,* complete with chaos, destruction and unceasing screeching at high decibels. It wasn't for the faint of heart. "I guess you may have a point."

Jan didn't even try to not look smug. "I know I do."

All this maternal advice was wearing Evie out. It had been a long time since she'd had a heart-to-heart with her mother about anything, never mind raising her girls.

And all this advice made Evie uneasy—didn't her mother realize she made decisions regarding her daughters all the time?

Unable to sit still for a moment longer, Evie hopped up from her chair. "I'll go ahead and call August to tell him no, then."

"Evie Ray Randall, you'll do no such thing. You need to call him up, thank him for the invitation and say you'd love to go." Now her mother was giving her dating advice?

This was suspiciously starting to feel like high school. "But the girls—"

"Will stay here with me and Dad, and we'll all get along just fine." And with that, her mother smiled brightly, just like Carol Brady.

But they were not on a TV sitcom, and her problems were not about to be solved in thirty minutes. Nope. Evie didn't trust her own judgment, didn't know what she wanted and, furthermore, she was not going to do what her mother wanted and brightly smile and wait for the announcer to say tune in next week. "Mom, I don't know about that."

"That's because you're thinking too hard. Just enjoy yourself."

Enjoy herself. Hmm. Evie glanced at Missy, who was chewing on a plastic lid with the tenacity of a teething pup. "You're going to have teeth marks all over your Tupperware, Momma."

Jan grinned. "I'm going to love every one of them. It's been too long since things got a little mussed up. Now, go call August. Go say yes and be done with all this angst."

Angst? With some dismay, Evie realized her mother was right. She was inserting more drama into this situation than the average thirteen-year-old.

It was certainly disconcerting to be corrected by both her daughter and her mother. Evie stepped toward the phone, but not before pointing out the obvious. "This isn't technically a date. I'm not dating, period."

"It's a boat cruise, dear. That's dating in Bishop's Gate."

That's what Evie was afraid of. She was afraid it definitely was a date...and something more. Evie knew if she was out alone with August without any family to buffer their conversations, their night wouldn't feel simple and uncomplicated. It would feel like the beginning of something. The beginning of a relationship.

After giving Missy a washcloth to chew on from the freezer, Jan leaned forward. "Evie, have you gone out on a date with anyone since you know, you and John…" Her voice drifted off as if she was trying not to curse in front of her grandchildren.

"Divorced? Yes."

"And?"

"Well, it was only one date."

"And?"

Evie looked furtively at Missy before lowering her voice and telling the god-awful truth. "It sucked. I got set up with a friend's brother."

"Uh-oh. And since then? How come you haven't gone out?"

"Mom, where am I supposed to meet men? Over the phone at the catalog?" What Evie didn't say was that she didn't know what she'd do if a man asked her out, anyway.

"I bet you might meet some very attractive men over the phone," Jan said. "Although, I truly doubt that any of them would ever be as nice as you-know-who." Picking up the portable phone, Jan handed it to Evie. "Now go out on the back patio and call August. I bet he's just standing by the phone, waiting for your call."

"Yes, ma'am," Evie said, shaking her head as she did what she was told.

This whole situation was completely surreal. Imagine, she and August going on a tourist cruise. Getting nervous about it. The image of August eagerly waiting for her call.

That was the stuff of movies, not her life. Her life involved Lean Cuisines and dirty diapers and forgetting to do laundry.

Still not knowing what she was going to say, she punched in August's cell phone number and stepped outside into the blazing hot sun so no one would overhear her.

August answered on the first ring. "Evie?"

Score one for Mom.

"Hi. Listen. The girls don't want to go out on a boat," she said before they could start saying a bunch of useless things about the weather and how hot it was.

"Oh. Well, okay."

"But I do, if you want me." As her words echoed back to her, Evie closed her eyes in mortification. That did not come out like she'd intended. "I mean, if you'd like just the two of us to go. Still."

After a pause, he said, "How do you feel about that?"

"Good. I mean, okay. I mean, August, are you psycho-analyzing me?"

He laughed, rich and full and dear. "Never. There's a cruise that leaves at seven and comes back at ten. They serve fried shrimp and grilled chicken and fruity drinks with umbrellas. What do you think?"

Heaven. It sounded like heaven, and so good that she couldn't even bear to not think about grabbing hold of his offer with both hands. "I think if I'm going to drink anything with an umbrella, I'd best drink it with you."

"We can walk to the pier, if you don't mind a forty-minute walk. It takes just about that long to get there in traffic."

"I don't mind the walk at all."

"I'll pick you up at six. We'll take our time. I'm glad you decided to go, Ev. Because, well…I do want you."

And with that, he hung up. Making her feel all tingly and hot and bothered. Making her feel like she was at the top of the Ferris wheel and the power was off and she was swinging her legs like nobody's business.

Evie glanced at her watch. It was four o'clock. Two hours to get ready or back out. Glancing toward the beach, she watched a family of four clean up next to a newly formed sand dune. The dad was shaking out a blanket, while the mom was corralling kids.

As for the children, they looked sunburned and tired and happy. Just like she'd been every time they'd come here so long ago.

The screen door snapped open. "Did you make a decision?" her mom asked slowly.

"August is picking me up in two hours."

"I'm so glad. I always did think you and August had something special together."

"Mom, I'm not romantically interested in August." And she wasn't even going to think about her Freudian "you want me" slip.

"That's fine."

"I'm not interested in dating."

With a practiced eye, Jan looked to where Evie's attention had been just moments before. "That's a nice family. Reminds me of your dad and me. You and your brother never did want to go inside."

"John and I used to do things like that."

"Did you?" Her voice sounding faintly surprised, Jan said, "I seem to remember you talking about *hoping* you'd do things like that. Did you ever, Evie? Did you ever go on trips and sit on blankets and just be?"

Just like that, the dream evaporated as quickly as it had come. "No," she admitted. "John would get busy with work or I would find a dozen excuses for us not to go away together. Before we knew it, we'd be planning to do something next year."

In front of them, the husband looped an arm around his wife as they shuttled their two kids and a whole assortment of floats, blankets and toys back to their cottage. When they were gone completely, Jan shrugged. "I guess John's 'next year' finally came, didn't it?"

Thinking of the night John went from husband to ex in the space of ten minutes, Evie nodded. "It sure did."

WHEN AUGUST GOT TO THE Rays' cottage, he knocked on the door and was welcomed by a burst of voices and the blare of the stereo. He stopped short to see Jenna and Mike dancing to an old 1950s song. Jenna was sparkling, she was so happy, and kept whooping it up every time Mike twirled her.

"Hey, August!" Mike called out, twisting a little in his bare feet. "I've got my best girl here. We're rocking around the clock."

"But there's no clock!" Jenna said gleefully. "It's all about three-o'clock rock!"

Back in the kitchen, Jan was sitting with Missy and helping her sort a mess of animal crackers. "Hey, August. Do you want something to drink?"

"No thanks. I'm, uh, just waiting for Evie."

When Mike picked up Jenna and twirled her so fast she squealed, Jan laughed. "You being here is almost like old times, huh?"

"Almost," he replied with a smile. Back in high school, he and Evie would have never been caught dead dancing with her parents. But, he certainly had spent many a night waiting for Evie to get ready.

"Years ago you were a lot more talkative."

Years ago he wasn't nervous.

He'd been a teenager and cocky enough to think he knew how to do everything right. Cocky enough not to care if he didn't. Now, things were different.

Now he was worried about trying too hard or saying the wrong thing. "Is, uh, Evie ready?"

"She's downstairs, go check," Mike said, just as "Leader of the Pack" roared on.

August didn't need to be told twice. Quickly, he trotted down the stairs and was immediately surrounded by blessed silence. When he noticed that all four six-paneled doors were shut, he called out, "Evie?"

"In here."

He hesitated before opening her door. For some reason, it didn't matter he was almost thirty. He felt awkward and self-conscious entering her bedroom with her parents upstairs. He knocked.

"Come on in."

He turned the handle, then stood with a smile as she stood in front of the mirror, looking this way and that. "What do you think?" she said. "This dress is a little big…do I look like a hanger?"

Dressed in a pale blue cotton dress, the top fitted with short sleeves while the bottom folded out into a long, flowing skirt, Evie look feminine and pretty. "You look great."

She rolled her eyes. "Thanks. Do you think I need a jacket or something?"

"I don't know. There might be a breeze."

She grabbed a well-worn jean jacket. "I'll bring this just in case." Next, she slipped on a pair of fancy white leather flip-flops and treated him to a smile. "I'm sorry I made you wait."

"It's fine. I probably came here early."

The ceiling thumped. Looking up, Evie sighed. "When everyone gets going it just about drives me mad."

He laughed, liking her honesty. "It's pretty much *American Bandstand* up there. I was afraid they were going to make me join in and do the twist."

Her gaze flickered over his legs, making him glad she wasn't as immune to him as she liked to pretend. "You would have made a good addition."

"I'll take a rain check on it."

There went that pretty half smile. The one that almost met her melancholy eyes. Was she, too, thinking of things that could have been but never were? Stepping forward, he murmured, "I'll dance if you dance with me."

"Name the date and I'll be there."

August was tempted to do that, just to see what she'd say. But instead of pressuring her further, he just nodded. "I'll keep that in mind."

She met his glance, then looked away, swallowing hard. "Oh. Well. My parents love to dance with Jenna. She loves it right back." Evie shook her head as they headed upstairs. "I don't remember them ever doing those things with me, but I guess they did."

"What about you? Do you dance at home?"

"No," she retorted. A short laugh burst through, too, but it clashed with the worry in her eyes. "By the time I get home from work, feed the girls and get them bathed and ready for bed, the last thing I want to do is dance. Do you think that's bad?"

"No."

"Really?"

"Really," he said, throwing an arm over her shoulders like he used to do.

Slowly they climbed the stairs. The narrow stairwell had never felt so confining. August was aware of Evie's silky skin, of the light perfume she wore, of the birthmark she used to hate marking the back of her neck. Under his arm, he felt her body tense slightly, as if she was as aware of him as he was of her.

But then the music pounded at them again. When Jenna spied them, she dropped her grandpa's hands and scampered over. "You going, Momma?"

"Yep," she said pressing a kiss to Missy's brow. Missy blinked back solemnly. "'Bye, Miss."

She turned to Jenna, who was waiting for a kiss of her own. "And bye to you too, Miss JJ."

Jenna took a full two steps back. "You goin' with August?"

August heard the accusation in the seven-year-old's voice as clearly as if she'd knocked him upside the head with a bell.

Evie must have, too, because wariness flew back into her eyes. "We're just going on the boat trip I told you about."

"You're wearing a dress."

"Uh-huh."

"I think your mother looks pretty, Jenna," Jan said. "Come back and dance with us."

Out went her lip. "Daddy—"

"We'll call him tomorrow. 'Bye, now," Evie said firmly.

Evie walked to the door, but paused. August saw her look at her dad.

He winked. "It'll be fine, honey. Go on now."

"Have fun, don't rush home," her mother said. "We've got everything under control."

Jenna turned away, her shoulders stiff. Reaching out, August squeezed Evie's hand. "You ready?" he whispered.

Indecision faded into resolve. "I'm ready."

Then finally, the sliding glass door opened and shut, and they were walking on the path they did the first night Evie arrived. As he half expected, she immediately pulled off her sandals and scrunched her feet into the sand.

"I'm glad we're walking," she said. "I can't get enough of the feel of sand between my toes."

He couldn't get enough of watching her. "Careful now, people will think you're a tourist."

Evie laughed at that. "Better a tourist than a snowbird."

He pretended those were fighting words. "Watch your tongue, Evie Ray. Here at the Silver Shells we love snowbirds."

"You love snowbirds? When we were kids, I thought you called them winter interlopers."

"Now those snowbirds save my bottom line. I'm grateful for them, that's a fact."

"I guess so." She glanced sideways at him. "But still, I'll remind you of that in January." As if the thought pleased her, she added, "Hey, wouldn't it be something if I could get away then?"

"Why don't you?"

"Because I have a job and kids."

If August needed any more reminders about how different their reality was from his daydreams, that was it. Evie had a life. In Texas.

And it didn't involve him.

Chapter Eight

"I'll take your tickets," a lanky college-aged guy said as Evie and August finally made their way to the front of the line.

August handed him two bright orange tickets before stepping onto the sloped wooden ramp and reaching for Evie's elbow. "Careful," he said as his fingers curved around her arm. "It can be slick right here."

Evie appreciated his gallantry, though what she really appreciated was his touch. Even that one simple connection had her mind drifting back ten years, remembering just how mesmerized she'd felt when he'd caressed her bare skin. Truly, had anyone ever had as capable hands as August Meyer? Warm and large, competent and calloused. Strong and dependable. They were a symbol of everything he was…and everything John had never been.

As they made their way across the wooden plank and onto the deck, August turned to her. "Inside or out?"

"Need you ask? Outside, and near the front."

"Toward the bow," he corrected.

His familiarity with boating terms made her smile. "Did you take up sailing?"

"No. I've just been on my share of boats."

That made sense. After all, they were in Florida. But what wasn't quite as clear was why he chose their current activity. Out of everything they could have done...this wasn't what she would have expected.

"I have to admit that I'm surprised you wanted to go on something like this," she said. "I never pictured you enjoying sailing around the Gulf of Mexico with a hundred other people."

"Why?"

"It's awfully touristy."

"Yeah, but a lot of things around Bishop's Gate are." Pointing in the distance, he said, "Take the Ferris wheel, for instance."

She flushed just looking at the old brightly painted ride.

August continued, "I think you'll enjoy yourself tonight. There's a reason people pay big bucks for this cruise. It's worth it." He took hold of her hand and led her to an ornately decorated bar in the middle of the boat. "What will you have?"

Evie had been thinking of a cold Coors. But seeing the jungle decorations and the array of choices in front of her, she made a split decision. "I think I'll take a piña colada. I'm living on the edge tonight."

August grinned. "Make sure there's an umbrella in it, would you, Pam?"

Pam the bartender gave a mini-salute. "Sure thing, August."

As Pam turned on the blender, Evie turned to August. "Okay, fess up. Are you a regular here?"

"Almost. I'm the owner of a vacation resort. I can't count the number of guests I've booked reservations for."

"And sometimes you've accompanied them?"

Something flickered in his eyes as he replied. "Sometimes I accompany them."

When they finally had their drinks, they walked to a table marked "reserved."

And that's when Evie began to get the idea that maybe the whole evening wasn't as spontaneous as she'd thought. Soon after they closed the gate to the dock, their tour guide began to speak, gesturing toward life jackets and lifeboats. Evie listened politely, though she doubted she'd be able to tell another soul where to seek help if it was needed.

All that she seemed to be able to concentrate on was August and the casual way he sat, one foot resting on the back of a chair in front of them. The way he sipped his beer and raised it in greeting to a group of men at a table nearby.

Within minutes, *The Bishop's One* pulled away from the dock and set out into the warm gulf.

"How big is this thing, do you think?"

"A hundred feet, give or take."

"I guess it needs to be this big," she said as a three-piece calypso band started playing a bright, islandy steel drum song. "I mean, with the band going and all."

"Stop analyzing, Evie. Just relax."

Evie decided she was going to need another sip or two of her frosty drink to accomplish that. Her body was all keyed up…obviously reeling from the fact that she was out on a date for the first time in months.

Or maybe because she was out with August and he was looking at her like there was no one in the world he would rather be with.

"I spent yesterday with Tanya," she said as the boat picked up speed after gliding by two bright orange floating buoys. "We went shopping together."

"I heard Missy gave her quite a scare when y'all went to the beach."

Evie laughed at the memory. "It was so funny, August. Poor Missy was spitting sand and thoroughly miserable, and Tanya looked stunned and out of her league."

"I would have felt that way, too."

"I guess dealing with babies takes practice," Evie murmured.

"Tanya's time will happen soon, I imagine."

Evie noticed August didn't mention himself being ready for babies. For a moment, she wondered why she cared.

August stood up and grinned. "Look, Evie."

Bracing her hand on his shoulder, she looked over the railing and was instantly charmed. "Dolphins!" Evie watched as one, then two others, appeared, swimming side by side, then chasing each other through the bumpy currents.

Soon, a gasp surrounded them as other passengers spotted the dolphins and watched them frolic.

"I wonder where they came from?"

"I think they know the boat's schedules by heart. I haven't heard of a cruise where they weren't playing in the wake and being clowns."

Their tour guide called out warnings not to feed them, then began describing their ocean habitat. "They enjoy interacting with people, and travel in packs of four to six. Some of our guides have even recognized and named a couple of these fun animals."

August chuckled. "Our guide is Nathan Emory. He's pretty adept at making this little cruise sound like the adventure of a lifetime."

Evie thought his good looks and easygoing demeanor also served him well. "He's doing a great job."

"I think so, too. It's hard to maintain that fine line of being informative without boring the audience. No one comes on these twilight cruises for an oceanography lesson."

She did her best to look shocked. "Really?"

He laughed. "No one besides you, Ev."

The warmth in his voice matched the heat of waning daylight, and made her smile.

"I'm glad I said yes to this."

"Me, too."

The band behind them played an old Bob Marley song and with a flick of a switch, tinkling lights appeared on every rim of the boat, giving their cruise a magical touch.

Evie and August got another round of drinks, wandered to the open buffet and picked up a pile of cocktail shrimp, fried fish and hush puppies.

As the salty air blew in their faces, Evie knew she was in her own personal heaven. How else could she describe her feelings? She bit into the crunchy, warm hush puppy and groaned, earning an appreciative grin from August and a wave of embarrassment from herself. "Sorry. I know I learned somewhere not to groan while I ate."

"Groan all you want, baby."

Playfully, she tossed a celery stick his way. "You get this food all the time. I forgot how good it tastes."

"I'm glad it tastes good." Quietly, he added, "I wish it hadn't been so long since you'd had some."

Suddenly, Evie wondered where the years had gone. Maybe she should have taken Jenna to Florida more than just once. Maybe she shouldn't have waited for her parents to practically drag her butt out of Texas.

Nathan announced a few anniversaries, a honeymoon couple, and a woman's fortieth birthday. Fortified by their drinks, everyone dutifully sang a round of the Beatles' "Birthday." Then, as the band broke into a new set, a few couples began to dance on the small parquet floor.

"Want to dance?" he asked.

"Why not?" Evie said, walking into his arms just as the band switched to something a little more slower.

He held her securely, and not too close, with her right hand in his, and lightly clasping her waist. Beside them, a pair of twenty-year-olds were practically glued to each other, their bodies swaying in motion.

Evie found herself remembering another time, another lifetime, really, when she dared to wear tiny skirts and small T-shirts and high heels.

"I'm envious of them," she whispered in August's neck. "The girl looks so free and uninhibited in her boyfriend's arms." They looked like she used to feel—confident and pretty.

"You're not?"

"You know what I mean. No responsibilities, no worries about arm flab."

August unclasped his hand and ran his fingers up her arm. "All I feel is soft skin. If you're looking for someone to feel sorry for you, it won't be me," he teased. "I think you look great."

"Sorry. I didn't mean to sound like I was fishing, I guess I'm just trying to remember what it felt like to be so un-body-conscious."

"You mean before kids?"

"I mean exactly before kids." With a dramatic sigh, she looked up at him. "I'll never wear a bikini again."

"You don't need to." His green eyes darkened. "I remember exactly what you looked like in one."

And just like that, memories swam back. "I remember, too." When August raised his hand to the middle of her back and pressed her closer, she complied, feeling his muscles under his shirt. Remembering another time, when they'd danced, but were wearing far less.

The summer before her senior year, she'd been very fond of a tiny black bikini. Strapless and brief up top and almost all strings down below, her parents had threatened to not let her leave the house. But she had. The first time she'd worn it, she'd gotten sunburned in places that had never seen the sun.

She'd worn it the night they'd gone down to Cascade Beach with all their friends and had a bonfire near the rocks. They'd had s'mores and soda and a few snuck beers. Before long, she and August had taken a blanket and gone to Cascade Cove.

They'd kissed and touched and learned about their bodies. And before long, she hadn't even been wearing that tiny suit.

Against her will, her body reacted, warming her insides, making her feel almost sunburned once again.

"That was some night, wasn't it?" August murmured.

"It was." It had been everything she'd dreamed of and nothing she'd expected. "Just three nights before I left."

"I was so worried I'd gotten you pregnant."

"I was so worried my life was going to be over."

His hands tightened on her waist. "Would it have ended, Evie? If you had been pregnant, would you have regretted it?"

"I don't know. I was just really glad it had been a false alarm and my life went on as planned."

"It went so well, you never came back."

There was bitterness in his voice. Regret. She felt those same things, too, but she also felt honest enough with herself to have moved on. She couldn't afford to have regrets…how could she? With John she'd had Jenna and Missy.

"Never say never," she quipped as the song ended and by mutual agreement they wandered back to their table. "After all, I am here now."

The tension left his eyes. "You are. And you're here for a month."

Three more weeks.

A wayward seagull flew a little too close for comfort, its beady eyes examining her near-empty plate with interest. August laughed it off, waving the bird away with a hand.

She liked how he looked in his loose linen shirt, with the thin black and navy lines snaking down in wavy stripes. The first few buttons were undone, showing a few inches of his bare chest.

Evie tried not to notice that his skin looked as toned and smooth as it did back in their earlier days. Tried not to realize that she'd inhaled his skin, had feasted her senses on everything August while they were dancing.

"Yes, well…" she murmured. Meeting his eyes, she tried to smile. And because she didn't want to remember things that couldn't be again, she brought up the topic she usually tried so hard to avoid. "So do I look better than when I first got here? Everyone said I looked like hell."

"Oh, you still do."

"What?"

Humor flashed in his eyes. "Sorry, I couldn't resist. You do look good…and I never said you looked bad."

"What did you think?"

"That I was happy to see you after so many years. That I was happy to see the girls, too."

"I'm glad."

He leaned closer. "Would you like to see each other more often? Do this again?"

Well, she knew what she wanted to say. The part of her that hadn't had sex in two years was thinking seeing August all the time was a very good idea. The part that missed flirting and wearing tight skirts and low-cut shirts wanted to scream okay and ask for another fruity drink.

But that wasn't her now.

Actually, it hadn't ever really been. Had it? Wasn't that why she'd taken the safe route and gone to college near home and married John?

Safe John, who actually hadn't ended up being very safe?

"I'm not here for an affair," she blurted. Unfortunately, the hand she'd just slapped over her mouth couldn't take back her words.

"I don't recall asking you for one." He paused. "Did you think that was why I asked you out?"

If she could have jumped over the railing she would've. "No. Yes. I don't know. You're single."

"O-kay," he said slowly, as if he was testing every syllable. "Evie, I don't know where you're going with this."

"It is fun. And, I'm sorry. Obviously I need to learn my liquor limits."

August linked his fingers through hers. "I don't think it's the rum talking, Evie."

She didn't think it was, either. Mortified, she looked away, hoping against hope another group of dolphins would start jumping around…anything to ease the moment.

"But if I did want an affair, I'd choose you, Ev."

The words were so over-the-top, so out of character, so silly, Evie burst out laughing. "Thanks."

This was a good night out. She'd had a few fun drinks, and eaten more at one sitting than she had in months. She'd danced and seen dolphins. Felt the salty breeze skim her cheeks.

Felt August's hands along her back. Held his hand and laughed.

And for a split second, had remembered being the girl

she used to be. The one who wore tiny bikinis and danced and sang and had been totally, completely in love with August Meyer.

And had never been completely honest about that.

Hmm.

Chapter Nine

"John, this is such a surprise," Evie said the next morning as she was still trying to come to friendly terms with her first cup of coffee.

When her parents' phone rang and she'd picked it up, it had been the shock of her life to hear her ex-husband's voice on the other end of the line. "I didn't think I'd hear from you so soon. What are you doing home? I thought you said you were going to be gone for two full weeks."

"I know I did, but everything changed. After three days in Tokyo, one of the guys amended his recommendations for the business plan, which meant I had to go back to the corporate office and rewrite the damn thing. Again." She heard him sigh in frustration. "So, after flying twenty hours and being in Japan for a whole forty-eight, I got to get back on the plane and go back home. I finally arrived last night."

There was a wisp of an expectant tone in his voice, which in turn gave her a sinking feeling. *John wanted something.*

With nervous motions, Evie poured another generous amount of coffee creamer in her mug, topped off her coffee, then took both the phone and her liquid fortification outside. Her father was listening to her side of the conversation without a bit of embarrassment, and she wasn't ready to face both men at the same time.

"You okay, Evie?" Mike called out as she stepped through the screen door.

I'm fine, she mouthed, though she didn't feel that way at all.

As John droned on about slow baggage handlers, long customs lines and the lack of new in-flight movies, Evie scurried out to the patio, down the steps, and to what was becoming her favorite place to sit—the old iron chairs in the sand.

At the moment, she didn't even care that a pair of joggers on the beach could probably see how frumpy she looked, her hair hastily secured in a messy knot, her melon-colored pajama bottoms clashing with her bright pink camisole. When she realized John was waiting for some sort of response, she pulled out one she'd said innumerable times throughout their married life. "Good luck. I hope you get that report done in record time."

After a second's delay, he said, "You okay?"

"Fine," she chirped. Her voice was high-pitched and off-key. Slightly hysterical sounding.

Because Evie knew what was coming. Over the years, she'd developed a sort of sixth sense…predicting what John Randall was about to say.

It was ironic, actually, given the fact that he'd surprised the heck out of her when he'd asked for the divorce.

And, like the tide that was coming in at 9:14 a.m.—just as the paper predicted—John was almost ready to get to the real reason he'd called.

But still she stalled. "It's really pretty here. The sand is as warm and soft as I remembered, and the weather not too muggy. Jenna's having a ball."

He ignored that. "When do you think you'll be coming back?"

"Not for another few weeks, John. We just got here."

"Oh."

He'd sounded so taken aback, Evie felt as if she'd just won that wrestling match. *Score one, Evie.*

Maybe he hadn't developed the sixth sense that she had. The one that alerted her when things were about to get ugly.

"I don't want you to mess your trip up on account of me. But since I'll be in town and all…you won't stay there a whole month now. Will you?"

"Actually, I don't know why you'd want us to go back. We've got plans and such. The girls would be disappointed." Evie closed her eyes, because even to her ears, her reasoning sounded lame.

"But Evie, I'm here. In Grapevine."

She hated it when he sounded lonely. John was the one who'd left their marriage. Didn't he remember?

But instead of saying that, she sidestepped. "I can't tell my parents I'm going to leave early. They invited me out here and have activities planned."

"Maybe you should talk it over with the girls. If you told them I was home, alone…" His voice drifted off.

John sounded so pitiable that Evie snapped. "John, Missy won't be able to discuss this rationally for some time."

Heavy sigh. "You know what I meant. If you speak with Jenna, I'm sure she'd tell you that a month is a very long time to not see her father."

Score one for John. Make it two, because he'd had the surprise attack from behind. As two senior citizens cruised by on the boardwalk, their snowy-white walking shoes glistening in the sun, Evie gulped down the last of her coffee.

Now she was trapped. At the moment, she'd give anything to have another full cup in her hand. But Lord knew if she wandered back inside, still talking to John, either her dad was going to pull the phone away or Jenna was going to start crying for her daddy.

Then, the next thing Evie knew, she'd be talking about going home even though that was the last thing she wanted.

Because she couldn't do anything else, Evie dug her toes deeper in the warm sand and tried to stand firm. "John, Jenna has some pictures for you. We'll send them out in the mail this afternoon."

For twenty seconds, time stood still. "You're not going to come home?"

"I'm not going to change three people's lives just because you're lonely."

"I didn't tell you to leave."

"You wouldn't, John. You'd guilt me into it, and before I would know what was happening, I'd be doing everything I could to make you happy." Just like she'd used to do.

"Don't get emotional on me."

How could he even say that? It was *all* emotional. She loved the girls. He did, too. They'd had a relationship for almost eight years.

She was just attempting to stand on her own two feet. And even though she was momentarily sitting down, Evie knew she wanted to be able to stand up and not be hobbled.

"Are the girls around?"

He sounded so hopeful. He was a good father. But, at the moment, he was a hell of an ex-husband. Making her voice as syrupy as possible, she looked to either side of her on the beach. "Gosh, they're not. They must be doing crafts with Mom."

"Oh."

"We'll call you tomorrow, if you want," she offered, feeling magnanimous. After all, she had just won the battle. She was staying put, no matter how John felt about that.

There was a suspicious pause. Then he said, "Evie, you better not call tomorrow, I've got some plans."

"Oh, work?"

"No. I'm going golfing."

A purely evil thought crossed her mind. One that involved golf clubs and whacking him on the head. "Monday then."

"Yeah, give me a call on Monday at work. I'll stop whatever I'm doing and take your call."

How generous of him. "I'll talk to you then. 'Bye, John."

"Think about coming back early."

"I will." Well, she'd think it was the worst idea she'd ever heard. "'Bye!" She clicked off and leaned her head back with only a hint of regret.

"Crafts, Evie?" her mom said from behind her. "My goodness, I guess I'll go dig out the glue and pipe cleaners."

Either the sun had gotten really hot, or she was now blushing. "Mom. I didn't know you were there."

"After I heard the tone of your voice, I figured I better stick to the background. What did Prince Charming want?"

Prince Charming. They'd called John that from the moment they'd first met him and noticed his Disney clean-cut good looks. They'd teased her more often than not, calling her Belle and Sleeping Beauty and Cinderella, saying she was swept off her feet. "My prince's Asian trip ended unexpectedly early."

Jan sat next to her, carefully slipped out of her slides and placed two pedicured feet neatly on top of the sand instead of burrowing them deep like her daughter. "So he just wanted to check in?"

Her mother was way too transparent. "Since you were listening, I'm giving you no points for evasive maneuvers."

She snapped her fingers. "Darn. Well?"

"He wanted me to come back early. He said he only encouraged me to go because he wasn't going to be in Grapevine. But now that he is, he wants to see the girls."

"That's not your problem."

Evie had never heard her mother sound so uncaring with anyone. "No, no, it's not. But I can see his point."

"I do, too. And that point is just as egotistical as it was when we were planning your wedding." Scowling, Jan added, "He always was too full of himself."

The wedding! "Oh, no. We're not going to talk about the wedding again."

"I liked rose," her mother said, bringing up the color of Evie's bridesmaids' dresses for something like the three hundredth time. "You did, too."

"Just because he wanted navy bridesmaids' dresses—"

"That's another reason I should've been skeptical of him. What kind of man cares about such things?"

John. John had always cared about the details. The price of meat at the grocer's. The way the dry cleaners pressed the cuffs of his dress shirts. "I told him no."

"I know that dear. Your rose dresses turned out lovely."

"I told him no about coming back early."

To Evie's dismay, her mom looked surprised. "You did? Well, good for you."

"Not really, I felt like I was ripping a hole in his heart."

"He deserved it."

"Mom, I don't know about that."

"How did he take the news?"

"About how you'd expect. Not well."

"He'll get over it."

"I hope so. Uh, that's why I told him you were busy with the girls. He wanted me to ask Jenna and get her opinion."

Her mother, as she'd hoped, was dutifully horrified. "Jenna would hear her dad's voice and start crying."

"And then he'd do something like offer her a dozen stuffed animals or Legos or a new American Girl doll."

"And she'd be putty in his hands."

"Yep. Though, it's not really fair of me, is it? I mean he loves those girls."

Jan hopped up and crouched down in front of Evie, looking her straight in the eye. "You do, too. You've made every possible sacrifice for them."

"I know, but—"

"No buts, Evie. John divorced you and took away your life. You lost your house. Now, you don't do anything but work and care for the girls."

And not herself. "He did give me alimony. I get child support, too. He's not heartless."

"No, he's not. But he's manipulating you. And worse, he's manipulating the girls. He can just cool his heels for once in his life."

Because she wasn't as nice as she wanted to be, Evie said, "He won't cool his heels much tomorrow, he's playing golf. I have a feeling he's probably going to see that new gal Jenna said he's introduced them to. Terri."

"See?"

For almost the first time, she did. "Absolutely."

Jan picked up Evie's empty cup. "Just because it's

been such a trying morning, I'm going to make you a fresh pot of coffee."

Her mother had always known what to say. Wrapping her arm around her mother's waist, Evie leaned close. "Thanks, Mom. Thanks for butting in."

She laughed. "Anytime, dear. Anytime at all."

Chapter Ten

"What do you know about Harmonious Haven?" August asked Tanya as they walked through a unit before a showing.

Tanya flashed a light into the upper corners of the master bedroom closet, checking for spiderwebs. "Not a lot. Just that if we click into the site and type in 'Beverly Meyer,' Mom pops on."

"You've visited the site?" So far, August hadn't had the nerve to do anything but complain about the dating service.

"Yeah. Haven't you?"

"No."

"You really ought to at least take a look at HH, August. It's actually very informative."

"I can't do it. So, what does Mom look like? Is her picture any good?"

"She looks real pretty. She went and got a glamour shot done for her bio page."

His mother dolled up in lipstick and sequins made him feel all squeamish inside. "No way."

Tanya laughed. "Yes way. But there's no feathers or anything, it's tasteful," she added, reading his mind.

"Mom has on her lime-green sweater set, navy slacks and daddy's pearls."

That strand of pearls had belonged to their dad's mom. Now August felt annoyed that their mother was using them to seek other men. "I don't think she should be wearing them."

"I don't think so, either, but what can you do? They are her pearls."

"And they're on the Internet," he said, like robbers were scoping out Harmonious Haven just to plan their next heist.

"It doesn't matter, August. Mom looks pretty."

He had to ask. "Has she gotten any takers?"

Tanya sent him a withering glance. "Takers? August, do you mean dates? This is our mother we're talking about."

Save him from the semantics lesson. "Yes I mean dates. Does she? Has she?"

"Actually, no. Well, at least, I don't think so."

"I wonder why?" Perversely, August went to his mother's defense. "You know, she looks really good for her age."

"I agree."

"She's a lot slimmer than most other women, and her hair looks good, too." He'd been just thinking the other day that the short, pixie cut made her look youthful, though far different than the mom they'd grown up with. That mom had longer hair. It had always been perfectly styled and hair-sprayed stiff—like a helmet. Now she looked...*hip* wasn't the word, but it was close.

"Yeah, Mom looks great."

"So what's the problem?"

"I don't know. You have to fill out a personality profile. I haven't gotten up the courage to read it, but maybe I should." She paused on the stairs. "Maybe it needs some work."

August walked down the stairs and through the living room without much more than a cursory glance. "I bet you're right. Mom's so modest, she'd be the type to say that she does charity work instead of heading up whole organizations."

"Or that she enjoys a little ballet, not that she used to own a dance studio."

August pulled out his laptop, set it on a counter and logged in. "Let's go see what she said," he muttered, already typing in *www.hhmatch.com.*

Tanya raced over and pressed Delete before he could finish. "Maybe we should rethink this. Give her some privacy."

"You've already seen her photos, Tanya. I think you're being ridiculous."

"I know. But—"

"August, Tanya? Is that you?"

August quickly closed his laptop's lid. "Yeah, we're just catching up," he called out. "This unit has a showing in a couple of hours."

"Don't say a word about her dating," Tanya murmured before raising her voice as well. "We're in the kitchen, Mom."

Beverly joined them with a flourish—there was really no other good way to describe it. Her cheeks were pink, her eyes bright. "I've got news."

Tanya stood up. "What?"

"Two things. One…I have a date. Two, I just volunteered to help with the Star Spangled Fund-raiser."

August couldn't resist groaning. He honestly didn't know which was worse. The date…he couldn't even digest that one. And the fund-raiser he'd been through before. Many times. The fund-raiser was to help fund arts programs in Bishop's Gate, and their mother seemed to be chairing it almost every other year. "I thought you were going to take a break from fund-raising."

"I thought I was, too, but then I decided it would be best to keep busy."

"It's really stressful, Mom. Don't you think you had better wait until you see how your health is doing?"

Some of the girlish glow was replaced by iron will. "My health is fine."

"Your heart?"

"August, I did not have a heart attack. I had a procedure done."

"But your cholesterol—"

"It's lower, too." She put her hands on her hips. "Honestly, sometimes I don't think you listen to a word I say."

"Uh, why don't you tell us about the good stuff. What's this about a date?"

"A very nice man saw me on Harmonious Haven and asked if he could call."

Tanya actually clapped. "That's great!"

August got to the point. "When did this happen?"

"Two days ago."

"This is so exciting," Tanya said. "I bet that man couldn't resist your glamour shot."

August glared at his sister. "I thought these things took time. Aren't you worried about who this man could be?"

"Not particularly."

"You should be."

Tanya kicked August under the table.

"Mom, would you like us to check him out, just to be on the safe side?" August leaned down to rub his shin.

"No, I would not." Beverly hesitated and then blurted out, "My date is with Wayne Peterson! Remember Wayne?"

August turned to Tanya. "No. Do you?"

"Dr. Peterson?"

"Come now, Tanya, I don't think you have to address him as that."

"Who is he?"

Tanya turned to August. "You never had to get braces. He was my orthodontist."

Beverly smiled at Tanya. "He did do a very good job on your teeth, dear."

"What was he like?" August asked.

"I don't know. Old."

"He's my age. Well, one year older."

"He seemed really old," Tanya said.

"His wife divorced him after thirty years of marriage. Can you imagine that? Wayne saw my profile and e-mailed me privately. He said he didn't realize I was interested in dating already."

"*So soon.* That's what he meant, right? He didn't realize you were ready to date so soon after Dad died?"

Tanya winced. "August."

But his mother stepped forward. "What was that supposed to mean, son?"

Uh oh. August wished he could erase this whole conversation from his memory. Maybe even get hit with a load of bricks.

Actually, anything would be better than to be treated with the withering, hurt glare she'd mastered by the time he was four years old.

And, just like in his formative years, he was no match for it. "Nothing."

"It sounded like something." She narrowed her eyes. "Are you saying that even though you funded my online dating, you were sure I wouldn't get a date?"

"No, ma'am."

"What did you mean?"

"Nothing." When she continued to glare, he began to sing like a canary in prison. "It's just that Dad hasn't been gone all that long and you had a really good marriage—" He couldn't complete his thought. He really couldn't. So, he just let the thought hang there, in all its glory. A mess.

"Ignore August, Mom," Tanya interjected. "You know how he gets."

"I know no such thing. I know that I haven't forgotten your father. I know that I still miss him."

"We miss him, too," August said.

Shaking her head in frustration, Beverly let him know that once again, he was way off target. "August, I'm trying to say that while I still miss your father, he's gone."

"We know that, Mom."

"Do you? Sometimes I'm not sure. I was married and pregnant at your age, Tanya. And when I was your age, August, your father and I were looking at preschools." Neatly turning the tables, she said, "Why haven't either of you become involved in a committed relationship?"

"I did date Erin."

"She's a nice girl. You two could have been married if you would have committed. Why didn't you propose to her?"

Because he had worried that he would've just settled, like Evie so obviously had. "You know that answer, Mother."

"I dated Charley for five years," Tanya said, doing her best to divert their mother's attention.

"I never liked Charley." Before Tanya could say a word, their mom added, "I'm not saying I'm going to marry Wayne Peterson. I'm just glad to have someone to meet for coffee."

There was real pain in his mother's voice. August closed his eyes, realizing that once again, he'd been thinking of himself and his feelings, and not his mother's. "I'm sorry, Mom. I'm happy for you."

Her lip trembled. "I'm sorry for snapping at both of you. Inside, I'm all excited and a bit scared, and those emotions feel strange. I never thought I'd feel this way again."

Tanya gave her a hug. As August watched the two of them together, he realized how alike they both were. Years of ballet and dance had given them both a grace and strength that had served them well.

"Just let us know how we can help, Mom," he murmured. "You know we both want you to be happy."

"Thank you for that."

Minutes later, she left, Tanya by her side. When the front door shut behind them, August stared at the closed laptop and felt a new awareness. Life was full of unexpected occurrences. And once again, he was the one playing it safe.

Chapter Eleven

"You didn't have to come with us, but I'm glad you did," Evie said to August as they made their way to Corn Dog on a Stick with the girls.

Jenna walked beside them, more or less. Her favorite game was to run onto the sand dunes to find shells, inspect them all carefully through the violet lenses of her princess sunglasses, then place the keepers in the little canvas bag she wore diagonally across her shoulders. Missy seemed content to watch the world from her stroller.

August looked surprised at her words. "Are you kidding? I love corn dogs." Catching Jenna's eye, he added, "The more the better."

Jenna almost smiled before remembering herself and glared. Evie sighed. Her little general was still obviously not embracing August's role as her mother's new friend and was making sure Evie was completely aware of her feelings.

The curly ends of her braids flew up as she skipped forward, her pink-and-white sandals clipping along the planks of the boardwalk. "Momma said I could have two if I wanted."

"Do you think you can eat two?" August asked.

She paused to consider his question. "I don't know. Can you?"

"Yep, but I'm bigger."

Evie fought to keep her expression neutral as Jenna's smile almost appeared again.

"Momma, what about you?"

"I'm a one-dog woman, myself."

August chuckled as Jenna ran ahead. "You think she's ever going to smile at me again?"

"Maybe. I'm afraid she's become a little territorial. John's always divided his time with the girls, either with work or girlfriends. I'm afraid I've kept the rest of my life out of the picture when they're around."

"So they're not used to sharing you at all."

"Not even a little bit." Thinking how much her parents' gentle guidance had helped Jenna, Evie said, "Things are getting better. Believe me, I'm glad you accompanied us."

"Me, too. I've been so busy in the office, I've hardly been outside in days. Thanks for calling me."

They had to stop to let Jenna sort through a handful of shells. August touched Evie's shoulder. "So, how's your week been?"

"Good." She shrugged. "Really good."

August had noticed Evie no longer had that pinched, worried look she'd seemed to wear like a badge of honor when she'd first arrived. Maybe the Florida air and lifestyle was suiting her. "That's good to hear. I meant to call you, but the days just got away from me." That wasn't the truth at all. He'd enjoyed her company so much on the cruise that he was afraid he would say something too strong and scare her off if he took her out again.

"What's been keeping you busy—work or your mom?"

The question was vintage Evie. She'd never been one

to shy away from uncomfortable topics, either for herself or him. And because her directness was a nice change of pace in his life, he answered her as honestly as possible. "Both. Room reservations are a little down this year, I don't know why. Last year I already had Labor Day weekend sold out by the Fourth of July."

"How full are you?"

"Seventy-five percent."

"Are you worried?"

"Not yet." He shook his head. "Sorry. Let me be honest. I am worried, but it's not keeping me up at night yet."

"Not all night."

He laughed. "I guess your observation skills are pretty good, too."

"Yep. Now tell me about your mom."

He liked her honesty. "What have you heard?"

"All kinds of things."

Those gray eyes positively sparkled. Warily, he said, "From whom? Tanya?"

"And my mom." She waited two beats. "Beverly's been calling and giving Jan the scoop."

"She's planning a gala."

"I know that. That's old news, August. Tell me about her love life."

He waved a hand. "She's dating Dr. Peterson."

"Tanya calls him that, too."

Her lips twitched, making August realize once again that he was going to have to get a grip on his mother's active social life. "He was Tanya's orthodontist."

"What's he look like?"

"I don't know. I'm surprised you and Tanya haven't gone on Harmonious Haven and looked him up."

"We tried. You have to have an access code."

August noticed that Evie wasn't wearing a trace of

guilt. "I'm surprised you haven't found a way around that."

"Hush. I think it's nice that Beverly's dating."

"Do you?"

"Sure, I do. A woman wants to feel attractive and wanted, no matter what she's been through."

As soon as the words were out, August felt a change in the air that had nothing to do with salty breezes or the hot rays of the sun beating down upon them. A tension had formed between them, and it had electrified their conversation.

"Are you feeling that way, Evie? Have you forgotten what it feels like to be wanted?"

After fussing with the top of the stroller, Evie said, "We're talking about your mom."

"And maybe you, too?"

"August."

Though he knew he was making her uncomfortable, August pressed. He cared about her; she had to know that. He cared enough to risk her irritation. "After everything you've been through with John, do you have your doubts?"

Hurt filled her eyes, revealing the truth, and her pain.

Now August wished he could take his questions back. Of course she felt that way. Now he had to go and embarrass himself—and her—by making her admit it? "Never mind. I don't know what I was thinking."

"Fine," she replied, in a very un-Evie-like way.

Well, now he'd really done it. She'd shut down on him, her face an impassive mask. August wondered how he'd stayed so stupid and still gotten as old as he was.

Luckily, Jenna came running over to save them from themselves. "We're here, we're here!"

Sure enough, they were within running distance of the

infamous Corn Dog on a Stick. Located on the end of Jersey Pier, the bright yellow and lime green striped hut had been a teen hangout for as long as he could remember. He and Tanya had begged to go there after good report cards, he and Evie used to walk down to the Dog for lunch after swimming in the ocean for hours.

"Stay with us, Jenna," Evie warned, reaching out to touch her daughter's shoulder. "The planks are uneven, I don't want you to fall."

"I won't," Jenna said, but amazingly, she stayed with them, hopping and skipping over the lumpy planks. All the while, her eyes were focused on the striped awning ahead of them. "You sure I'm going to like 'em?"

"No, I'm not sure," Evie said. "But I hope you will."

"What about Missy?"

Bending down, she looked at Missy, who was observing everything with her big blue eyes. "Hungry?"

Missy ignored her, pointing instead to a man walking a beautiful golden retriever that had a worn red Frisbee hanging from its mouth. "Dop."

August laughed. "Pretty dop."

"Dog," Jenna enunciated. "Golden dog."

"Golden retriever," August corrected, since everyone was submitting their two cents. "And, I just happen to know its name."

"You do?"

August felt as if he just won the lottery. Finally, an open, sweet smile from Jenna, the obstinate. "It's Sam."

Jenna screwed up her face. "Really?"

"Really." Placing his hand over Evie's on the stroller, August murmured, "Do you mind if we go meet Sam?"

"Not at all. I think it's an excellent idea."

He smiled in return. A beautiful, gorgeous smile that had evidently never needed any help from Dr. Wayne

Peterson. And, taking her hand in his, he guided them over to Sam and the athletic guy who was standing with him.

"Hey, Chris."

"August, you got your hands full today."

"Meet Jenna and Missy and Evie."

"Nice to meet you," Evie said, liking the way August always put the girls first. She also noticed that he was still holding her hand, as if he was showing Chris that she was taken. That almost made her forget that he'd asked her about feeling vulnerable. "We've been admiring your dog."

Sure enough, Jenna had edged closer and closer to Sam and was obviously using every bit of self-control she had not to reach out and pet him. For his part, Sam eyed the girls with pleasure, his tail wagging in anticipation.

Chris knelt down on one knee, effectively putting him at Sam's sitting height and Jenna's standing one. "Would you like to pet him?"

Jenna nodded.

"Sit and drop, Sam," Chris commanded. Obediently, Sam dropped the Frisbee and sat before them.

"Dop! Dop!" Missy kicked her legs.

Evie knelt down, too, and unbuckled Missy, then held her so she could touch Sam. "Careful. Gentle, honey."

Jenna had a look on her face that could only be described as glee, as she stroked Sam's side. As if Sam knew he had two little girls in need of some love, he turned his head and gave Jenna a swipe across her cheek with his doggy tongue. "Oh!" she said, clearly thrilled. "Sam likes me!"

"He does," Chris agreed with a smile. "Sam only kisses new friends."

Jenna launched herself at Sam and wrapped her arms around his neck, her fingers sliding into his silky fur. "Sam!"

Evie stepped forward. "Jenna, careful. You can't grip a strange dog so tightly."

"It's okay, Evie," Chris said. "Look at Sam."

Sure enough, the golden retriever was eating up the love and affection like a new bone. His eyes were half-closed, and his tail continued to wag.

As Evie tried to coax Missy's pats into something more gentle, August caught up with Chris. It sounded as if Chris was something of an electronics expert, and installed sound systems in various buildings and houses around Destin and Bishop's Gate.

"Guess what? We're going to get dogs to eat!" Jenna said, laughing at her own joke.

Chris played along and pretended to look horrified. "Don't listen, Sam."

That made Jenna laugh even more uproariously. "They're not real dogs! They're *corn* dogs!"

"Let's go get them," Evie said. "Thanks for letting us see Sam."

"Anytime." Turning to Jenna, he said, "You all are friends now, so be sure and say hi to Sam next time you see us."

Jenna nodded solemnly, her little pigtails bopping with the motion.

Missy, of course, was tired of sitting, so Evie held both of her little hands as Missy tried to walk on the boards.

The smell of waffle cones and saltwater surrounded them, the mixture of scents unique to ocean boardwalks everywhere. Kids ran up and down the pier, their footsteps and shrieks blending and echoing with the sound of the surf.

In a way, it all felt cleansing and free, like time was suspended, and deciding how much to eat was all that mattered.

"I'll take the stroller, Ev," August said.

Then they were all at Corn Dog on a Stick, ordering up a mess of corn dogs, one cut up for Missy. After parking the stroller, August picked up mustard and ketchup packets, then directed everyone to the umbrella-covered tables nearby.

Finally, Evie bit into her own personal bit of heaven. "Oh, I forgot how good these are."

Jenna ate hers a little more skeptically, but then soon was halfway through one. "I like these, Momma. I wish we had these in Texas."

Evie shared a smile with August. "They wouldn't be the same. They're our vacation food."

After another bite, Jenna pronounced, "I like vacation food."

"Me, too, squirt," August said.

To Evie's pleasure, Jenna treated August to a genuine smile, showing everyone that she'd finally decided that she liked August very much.

As Evie sipped her lemonade, a trio of seagulls circled low, bringing squeals from Missy and a fresh burst of laughter from Jenna. It was a perfect afternoon.

TWO HOURS LATER, THEY arrived back at the cottage, tired and sandy. After eating, they'd gone to the children's area at Cascade Beach and let Jenna run around on the playground while Evie pushed Missy on the baby swing.

Then they'd dipped their toes into the water, which delighted Missy to no end, hunted for seashells and built a sand castle. After another hour they walked home, which seemed to take twice as long, especially with Jenna complaining that her legs hurt.

August saved the day by carrying Jenna on his shoulders, the seven-year-old finally dropping the last bit of her reticence around August.

When they arrived at the cottage, Jan was a lifesaver as she took hold of the girls and coaxed Evie to go sit with August out on the back patio.

When August offered to get them drinks, Evie wandered the patio and sat down to wait for him. The fan was on, cooling her pink cheeks, tempting her to close her eyes for a moment.

When she opened them, August was standing before her, holding two plastic tumblers filled to the brim with iced tea. His presence made her feel so many things—she half yearned to grab hold of his hand, and half hoped she could push him far enough away that he'd leave her alone.

"Do you have time for this?" she asked.

"Enough."

"I bet we're cutting into your work time."

"I'd rather be with you and the girls." Chuckling, he said, "I haven't had a corn dog in years."

"I guess even when you live here they're for vacations, too?"

"Definitely."

By mutual agreement, they wandered over to the sunken chairs. As naturally as if he did it all the time, August shrugged off his white T-shirt before leaning back against the sun-heated metal.

Evie tried not to notice. Tried not to notice just how ripped his stomach was. Even after all these years, he still sported a six-pack. Only now there was a very visible line of light blond hair snaking down the center of his belly, drawing her eye to his bare skin, forcing her to look away when her eyes drifted lower to his waistband.

Hold, now!

It had been a long time since she'd noticed anything like that. Over the years she'd taken John's physique for granted, imagining that he probably did the same with hers.

Of course, that hadn't worked out too well. John had lost interest. And, from what she understood from Jenna's reporting, John's interest had been rekindled with Terri.

Seeking to temper the awareness between them, Evie said, "I'd take my shirt off, too, but I think it might be a bit shocking for everyone here."

His green eyes flashed. "Not for me. Take whatever you want off."

Well, that only increased the heat between them. "Maybe I'll save that activity for another time."

"I'll look forward to it."

Behind them, Evie heard her mom talking on the phone, Jenna's high-pitched voice and the comfortable drone of the Cartoon Network. "So. Well. Thanks again for going down to the boardwalk with us. The girls loved seeing Sam."

"He liked seeing them, too. You ought to give them a dog."

"Yeah, that will be the day…one more thing to take care of."

"Maybe when Jenna's old enough to actually take care of a dog and not just say she will." Raising an eyebrow, he asked, "Do you think that day ever comes?"

"I couldn't tell you."

"I kind of doubt it. Back when I was growing up, I constantly said one thing and did another."

"We all did, I guess. Ben and me always said we'd help with the dishes and then forget to do them hours later."

"Tanya and I did that with sweeping the floors."

"For someone without kids, you sure got their number," Evie teased.

"Hey, I was a kid once. I didn't forget everything."

She chuckled and playfully nudged him with her shoulder. "Sorry, I almost forgot."

It seemed the most natural thing in the world for August to slip his arm around her just then.

And it seemed almost natural for her to lean a little closer to his bare chest and to place a hand right over his heart. "Finally," he murmured, curving his other arm around her. "I didn't think this day would ever come."

That little telltale comment should've sent up warning signs. Should've made her a nervous wreck, because even though she'd been finding herself very, very attracted to him, his whole presence in her life was still something of a surprise.

August leaned closer, his breath against her neck doing all kinds of things to the rest of her body. Making her extremely aware of his scent, and of her heart beating.

The way they still felt so good together.

And then, it seemed quite natural for August to kiss her. Right then. Right there. On her parents' back porch, in full view of the rest of Bishop's Gate.

With his shirt off and her toes gripping the hot sand for all she was worth. And her hand on his heart, where it was beating slow and sure.

While hers was going crazy because his lips were firm and perfect and he tasted like August and nothing had ever felt so good.

"Mmm," she groaned, pressing herself a little closer. August tilted his head, fingered her cheek and made her feel like she was the only woman in the whole world.

And then, like a spark in the sky, it was over and done with in a heartbeat.

Oh. My. Word.

Chapter Twelve

Evie didn't know how her dad did it, but inevitably, he always picked the best time in the world to ask her if she wanted to go for a walk—whenever her spirits were low or when things seemed too overwhelming. Whatever the case, she'd learned from an early age to always accept his offer.

When she was little, they took the same route around the neighborhood. First passing the Harpers' Doberman, then ducking under the Wilsons' pine that always needed trimming. Turning right at the Olsons' tudor with the inevitable new car in the driveway, and finally right again at the Barnhardts' fence that had once been stained dark brown but had for years simply just looked old.

Over the years, their routes changed. They walked the mall, the park near her dorm at A&M. The bike path near the house she lived in with John.

But her favorite place to walk with her dad had always been the beach in Bishop's Gate.

Holding a new cigar that her dad tried to sneak but everyone knew he smoked, Mike gestured to the back porch. "Are both girls napping?"

"Yep."

"Your mom's doing laundry. How about we get out of here for a little bit?"

The pull to go was strong, but the ties of responsibility weighed on her mind. "I better not, Dad. Mom might need me."

"Going for a walk was your mother's idea."

Their walks had never been Mom's idea. "You sure?"

"Positive."

"Let me go get my shoes."

Like a kid given an extra recess, Evie scurried down to her room, grabbed some socks and her sneakers, and stopped at the laundry room.

Jan looked at what she was carrying and smiled. "Going for a walk?"

"You sure you don't mind?"

"Not at all." Wrinkling her nose, Jan added, "Besides, your father's been dying for an excuse to smoke one of those cigars. Go make him happy."

"I'll be back soon."

Jan finished folding a golf shirt then looked up. "Don't hurry. I told Jenna we'd make pizzas out of refrigerator biscuits when she woke up. If you show up, she'll think it won't be a surprise."

"Yes, ma'am."

"Go on, now."

Evie scurried back up and was pleased to see that her dad already had on a pair of spiffy silver Nikes. "Fancy shoes, Daddy."

"White's out for men. Have you heard?"

To even think of her father following fashion trends made her smile. "No, but I'll take your word on it," she said, sitting down on a kitchen chair and slipping on socks and her favorite running shoes.

Her dad pretended to be blinded. "Lime green?"

"I'm not into white shoes, either."

After pausing at the door for her dad to light his cigar, they were off. "You're the only person I've ever heard of who can smoke and exercise at the same time."

"Oh, I don't smoke these every day, only about once a week."

They walked down the steps, crossed over to where the iron chairs sat, then scampered down the hill to the board-walk. It was four o'clock—that perfect time when there was a lull on the beach. Vacationers were getting cleaned up from being out all day, and locals were just getting home from work. In two more hours, the area would get crowded again, and be filled with the sounds of laughter and children shrieking.

"How did you know I was ready for a walk?"

"I didn't. I just wanted company while I enjoyed my cigar."

"Daddy."

He rolled his eyes. "I saw you and August last night."

"Kissing?"

"Yep."

"What did you think?"

He raised an eyebrow. "We're both a little too old for me to be thinking anything about you kissing, don't you think?"

"No. You've never been shy with your opinions."

He puffed a little longer. "I imagine you're right about that. Well, then. I guess I'd have to say it made me feel a little bit nostalgic."

That was the very last thing Evie thought she'd hear from her dad. She would have expected shock. Concern. Heck, even amusement that she was once again having a summer romance.

But nostalgic? It sounded almost like he was glad. "I don't know if I'm serious about August."

"You don't have to be. I'm thinking everyone needs to test the waters every now and then."

This conversation was a wealth of surprises. "Do you think August is serious?"

He pointed to her with the lit end of the cigar, the bright orange tip looking for all the world like a teacher's pointer. "Truth?"

She held up her pinky. "Always."

"Yes."

And that answer made all the lies she'd been telling herself for twelve hours fall to the wayside. "I think so, too, Daddy."

He looked pleased to hear her old name for him. With a sigh, he took another puff, then motioned her to follow him on a narrow path near a row of limestone boulders. After a time he said, "I guess the question is…what do you want to do about it, sunshine?"

"I don't know. I like August. I've always liked him."

"In a different way than that damn John?"

Oh, the way he said "that damn John"! It would have made her laugh if she wasn't thinking about him in the same way at the moment. "I don't know if it's different or not."

"Sure you do."

"Okay. With August, it's all feelings," she said, trying her best to describe a wealth of mixed-up emotions succinctly. "August makes me laugh, he makes me feel good inside. I feel happy and optimistic when I'm with him."

"And John?"

She paused to consider. "With John, everything was cerebral. I thought I should be happy with him. I thought we would be good together. I knew he'd make a good father. But even though everything looked right and sounded right, it all seemed just a little off-kilter. Does that make sense?"

Her dad moved his hand from side to side. "Kind-of-sort-of." After taking one final puff, Mike carefully tamped out what was left of his cigar then neatly deposited it a trash bin. Next, he bought two bottles of water from a beach vendor, handed one to Evie, then chugged the majority of his water in three gulps. After throwing out the empty bottle, he flexed his fingers. "I think I'm ready to go a little faster now."

Frustrated and confused by her feelings, but amused as all get out by her father's familiar antics, Evie lifted up a heel and stretched her quadriceps. "I'm ready, too."

"Let's go, then."

And off they went. Racewalking, they hopped off the cement path, scampered down a slope made up of crushed rocks and shells, then stepped down toward the beach, where the sand was packed so hard, it felt like cement underfoot.

They picked up the pace.

Now, as seagulls flew above them and a few shrimp boats and an offshore oil rig bobbed in the distance, no words were necessary. Nothing was but the familiar pace, the smell of the ocean, the hot beat of the sun on her shoulders and the trickle of sweat running down her back as she pushed herself even harder.

Ben and her mom had never understood their walks. Each had joined them through the years, but their company had felt wrong.

Jan Ray strolled. Strolled and chatted. She commented on fish, trash, cute bathing suits and the latest episode of *Oprah*.

Ben couldn't grasp the whole idea of walking together— every time they speeded up, he would break into a run or try to make it a race and act all important when he got home first.

After two miles, she and her dad turned around, then slowed their pace, just as two kids from the hotel part of Silver Shells raced out of their condos, pails and red plastic shovels in hand. Mike glanced at his watch. "Five-thirty. We're right on time."

Evie was panting so hard, she couldn't do much more than just nod. Her dad seemed to notice, because he purchased two more water bottles and pointed to a grouping of boulders near the entrance to the boardwalk.

Rubbing his leg, he grimaced. "My knee's barking. Let's give it a rest."

Evie sipped her water and thankfully sat down next to him. When she caught her breath, she finally said, "I've missed these walks."

"Me, too." Meeting her gaze, he murmured, "If you moved down here, we could do this all the time."

She tried to laugh off the invitation. "If I lived here, I bet we'd never make time to walk. We'd be running errands or working or whatever. You know that's what happens in real life."

"We still might be able to fit them in. You could move in with us for a while and we could help with the girls."

"You and Mom are a great help. The girls would love being so close to you, too."

"We'd love to see them more often."

"I have a job."

"You could get one here."

"Maybe." She paused. "I can't move them so far from John, Dad."

"John divorced you."

"But not the girls."

"As long as you stay so close to him, I don't think you'll ever move on."

"I have moved on. I'm here, aren't I?"

"Because John told you that you could go."

"I'm here because you asked. I'm over John, Dad. Haven't you been hearing me? I've been over him."

"Good. Because he didn't want you, Evie."

Oh, that hurt. It didn't matter that it was true. Maybe the words hurt *because* they were true. No one wanted to be anyone's discard.

Summoning up her courage, she said, "I know that, Daddy." But that admittance cost her just about everything. Against her will, tears pricked at her eyelashes. She blinked hard to keep them at bay.

No way was she going to shed another tear for John Randall. And certainly no way was she going to cry for him in front of her father.

Mike looked pained. "Shoot. Now I've really done it, huh? Your mother's going to kill me. Listen, I didn't mean it like it sounded. I didn't mean that you didn't deserve any better. You do, Evie." Crushing his plastic bottle, he tossed it into the trash can a few feet away. "That's what I'm trying to say. You've always deserved better than John Randall."

"If you've always thought so poorly of him, why didn't you ever say anything?"

"Maybe because I thought I was wrong? Evie, you were happy with John, so your mother and I didn't want to interfere, even if he wasn't our first choice."

"What was wrong with him?"

"Nothing."

"Dad."

"He never looked at you like August did," Mike finally said. "That summer before college, one day your mother and I were out for a stroll, and we saw the two of you together. You'd just gone to the pier for corn dogs or something. He was holding your hand." Mike paused. "He pulled you into a hug, and your mom and I saw his face. And that's when we knew."

Her dad's voice was soft and sweet. Almost wistful.

Evie was mesmerized by the story, never mind that it was about her. Leaning closer to the most important man in her life she whispered, "Daddy, what did you know?"

"I knew he loved you."

Her breath hitched. "Yeah?"

"August's face was so happy…happy to be near you. Happy to be holding you. It took my breath away. Hell, your mom and I went home and stayed up half the night, wondering how we were going to pay for college at Florida State."

This was news to her. "You would have let me go to Florida? Even though I'd already been all set for A&M?"

Mike hopped off the rocks and helped her down, too. Quietly, he said, "Did you ever look at August back then, Evie? Did you ever really notice how he treated you?"

"I…I don't know."

"I don't think you ever did," he said. "Because if you did, you would have realized that that boy would have hung the moon for you. All you would have had to do was ask."

As that settled in, her dad added one more thing. "Maybe you ought to do some thinking about that now. What are you willing to do? What are you willing to ask August to do? Because I tell you one thing, it's not about John Randall. At least, it shouldn't be anymore."

Evie figured it probably wasn't the best time to mention John's phone call.

"Thanks for the walk, Dad."

"Did I make you feel any better?"

As they headed back to home, Evie lied through her teeth. "Yep. I feel a lot better."

Pure relief flickered across her dad's face. "Good. Anytime you want to go again, let me know. Anytime at all."

Chapter Thirteen

Evie found August at the far back of the Silver Shells resort, glaring at an air-conditioning unit as if it was about to self-destruct in five minutes. "Do I need to call the bomb squad?" she teased.

His eyes lit up when he saw her, mirroring the way her heart did a little two-step whenever she spied his smile. "What are you doing out this way?" he asked, straightening up and wiping his hands on the edge of his T-shirt.

There was no reason to lie. "Looking for you."

Concern replaced pleasure in his eyes. Dropping the wrench he was holding into a toolbox, he stepped toward her. "Is anything wrong?"

"No. I was just out for a walk and saw your truck. And since we hadn't seen each other in a while, I decided to pay you a visit." Her voice drifted off as she heard her words in the open air. Hadn't seen each other in a while?

It had been a day and a half! Did she sound desperate?

But if August thought she was, he didn't let on, because he smiled again. "You picked a good time to find me. I've been standing here with these tools, wishing I knew what the heck I was doing."

"Things bad?"

"Bad enough." With a grimace, he pointed to the faulty air conditioner once more. "I had all the air conditioners serviced last month, but this one is already on the blink. The timing couldn't be worse, I'm supposed to fill this unit tomorrow morning."

"And it's only ninety-five degrees outside."

"Exactly." August frowned at the air conditioner. "A family reunion booked five of these condos, and picked our resort because I promised they could all stay next to each other. I've got to get this thing running or we're screwed."

His dilemma reminded Evie that there were probably a million little disasters like this in a week…yet he never complained about his job or the weighty responsibility. "If I could help you, I would."

"And here I thought you could do everything," he joked.

"I haven't mastered large appliances yet. Now if it was a toaster, no problem."

August laughed, the sound low and rich and making her feel eighteen again. "My loss then."

"What are you doing for dinner?"

He glanced over at her. "I haven't thought that far ahead. What about you?"

"The girls want to go to Rockin' Roberts." When she was a girl, she'd loved going to the Bishop's Gate landmark because the restaurant had giant statues that moved and talked and sang. Though the food was far from gourmet—mainly everything was fried—the place brought back good memories.

She'd been promising Jenna from the moment they passed the Florida state line that they'd go, eat fried shrimp and get their pictures taken with the costumed waiters.

Now, however, Evie was thinking that having August's company would make the evening complete.

And because all she was doing was thinking about their kiss and drinking fruity drinks on the back of a boat, she started talking fast. "My mom's already called Beverly. She and Tanya and some friend of Tanya's named Dan are coming, too. I wondered if you wanted to join us." There, she made it sound as if she wanted him there to be part of the group. Not there because she couldn't bear to be away from him for another twenty-four hours.

August stepped away from the air-conditioning unit just as she decided it wasn't very good manners to stand six feet from him while offering an invitation. Before she knew it, they'd gone from four feet to a slim fourteen inches apart.

Close enough to be thinking all about how things used to be. How they'd been just two nights before. Her breath hitched. She hoped he didn't notice.

But as a new awareness filled his gaze, Evie realized one thing…how could he not notice? At the moment, nothing seemed to exist but August. Nothing else really mattered but being near him again.

The feelings, so strong and unexpected, struck her like a gale force wind. When had she begun to live again? When had she stepped away from her past with John and started thinking about a future?

"Is that really why you walked all the way out here, Evie? To ask me out for dinner?"

"Not exactly."

"How exactly?" He took her hand, covering her fingers with his, making Evie remember that they'd really come a long way in a short time, relatively speaking. After all, she hadn't seen the guy in years. Hadn't thought of him in ages.

And now all she wanted to do was be by his side.

"So, why did you stop by?"

"I wanted to see you."

Satisfaction slipped in his gaze—there was no other way to describe it. "I've wanted to see you, too."

"Well, then." Suddenly, there was no past and no future. There was only now. That minute. That second. The way her hand felt in his.

The way he smelled so good and looked so familiar.

And right then, Evie's heart was beating a mile a minute because she wanted nothing more than to step a little closer to August and feel his lips against hers once more.

"I think there's something between us," she said, hating how husky, how desperate, her voice sounded. It sounded like she hadn't been near a man in years.

It sounded like she hadn't had sex in years. It sounded eerily like how she felt. Desperate and unsure. Anxious and wired. Eager and hungry.

And then she felt nothing but August's mouth on hers, whispering hello and everything that never needed to be said aloud.

She reached up and felt those broad shoulders, so defined by hours of swimming, and held on tight and kissed him back. Tongues and teeth and arms and fingers all got tangled up together.

Heat and friction and want ignited and burned, making Evie feel desired and full of fire. She held on to him for dear life, afraid to let him go, afraid that her reality would intrude again, and August and the wonderful way he made her feel would be gone in an instant.

When August lifted his head with a sigh, Evie had a feeling that he felt the same thing. After caressing her face with a slow gaze, he straightened and ran a hand through his hair. "So."

She smiled back. "So. I'm glad I came out to see you."

"Am I your summer romance, Ev?"

The words held a trace of irony, but she didn't think she actually heard regret. No, it was more along the lines of curiosity.

And because she didn't know what she wanted, only knew what she didn't want anymore, Evie sidestepped. "I don't think we have summer romances at our age, August."

"What do we have?"

She swallowed and tried to make a joke. "Plain old affairs?"

"Is that what you want, Evie?"

"I want to be close to you. I want to know that I'm going to see you on a regular basis without having to ask you out to dinner."

"What about later, when you go back home to Texas? What's going to happen then?"

"I don't know."

His lips quirked. "I guess we'll just figure things out as we go?"

He sounded impatient. Almost angry. His emotions triggered a like response. "Do we have to figure things out now? Damn, August. I mean, we just found each other again. Surely we don't have to make commitments... right?"

His muscles tensed. Everything in his body language told one story. Yes, he did want to make a commitment. Yes, he did want to make plans. Definitely. Without a doubt.

But instead of voicing those thoughts, he shook his head. "No. Of course not."

She pretended he was telling her the truth. "Good, because you were kinda scaring me for a minute there."

"Don't be scared." He turned, picked up a screwdriver from his toolbox and went back to the air conditioner. As he turned from her, Evie noticed a line of perspiration that had stained his T-shirt, burning a dark line straight down the middle.

Yes, it was hot, but was the heat suddenly affecting him, or was the conversation just as uncomfortable for him as it was for her? She reached to touch his arm. "Hey, can I get you a bottle of water or something?"

The muscle jumped under her fingers. "I'm okay."

"All right then. Well, I guess I'll just see you later," she replied, stepping backward. "I'll tell Jenna you'll be joining us. She'll be thrilled. She's really starting to like you."

"Is she? What would you tell Jenna if she saw us kissing?"

"I don't know. I guess that we are special friends. Old friends."

"Special friends? Old friends? Evie, I think we're more than that."

"August, I don't know what you want me to say." Thinking of her bossy daughter with the riot of red curls and the know-it-all attitude, Evie shook her head. "I can't read Jenna's mind, or make her feel things she's not feeling. Me having someone in my life is pretty new for both of us."

More softly, Evie added, "Don't worry. Jenna doesn't think too much about my social life, anyway. Her world mainly consists of grilled cheese sandwiches, *Dora the Explorer* and beach time."

He kissed her again, a quick brush of tender lips against her own, chaste by most standards, but terribly erotic by hers, if for no other reason than that they'd crossed into unchartered territory. "I've got to deal with some things, but then how about I pick you and the girls up?"

"I have car seats. I'll pick you up."

"I'll be waiting, then."

Evie barely heard him…she was already walking down the road. Away from his searching gaze. Away from all the things she was trying not to think about.

As August watched Evie walk away, he shook his head and called himself an idiot. What was he thinking, pressuring her like that? Did he want to lose her again, after he finally got her back in his life?

But maybe that was the point…did he even have her? A riot of emotions came flooding back as he recalled his childish dreams of her and their future together. He'd been so scared when he thought they were going to have a baby. But not scared of the responsibility, only scared of how he was going to make their future work.

Late into the night, he'd planned how he'd break the news to his parents, and how he'd go right to work at the resort, perhaps taking a class at the community college from time to time. He'd naively felt that they were right for each other, that everything was going to work out.

Then the bottom had fallen out of his dreams when Evie had called to relay the news. There was no baby, and no reason for them to worry about a future together.

Their "accident" could be forgotten.

A year passed. Though they'd only written each other a few letters during college, he'd kept an eye open as soon as Memorial Day passed, looking for their familiar station wagon.

He'd endured her brother, Ben's, sardonic looks when he'd appeared on their doorstep not two hours after they'd driven in. And had fought hard to keep from hitting the wall when Mike had told him that Evie hadn't wanted to leave her new boyfriend and was going to summer school with him. Finally August had had to come to terms with the fact that their relationship was over, and had been for quite a while.

He'd grown up a lot that summer. He'd dated as many beautiful girls as he could, joined a fraternity at Florida State and decided to embrace the whole college lifestyle, all the time knowing he would give it up in a heartbeat if Evie had contacted him.

But she never did. And he, like a fool, had always hoped. Even while he and Erin had gone out, August would catch himself comparing Erin to a girl he used to know. The girl he used to love.

Now he had Evie, but only for a short time. Her casual attitude was killing him.

But he'd be damned if she'd ever see that. This time, he was going to play it cool. He'd be whatever she wanted, and do his best to win her over.

His cell phone rang. "August, how's the unit?" Tanya asked from the front office.

"Not good."

"What do you want to do? Separate the group?"

"Nope. Give Bruce a call."

"He's going to cost a mint," she warned.

"I know, but we don't have a choice. The Baxter family is due in tomorrow by five."

Tanya whistled low. "Okay, I'll give him a call and call you back."

"I'll be waiting," he murmured as he clicked off.

Yep, he realized, after halfheartedly examining a few connections on the air conditioner, Bruce was definitely needed. And the guy would probably charge him double for an emergency service call.

Just one more thing in his life that hurt like the dickens but he hoped would be worth it.

Chapter Fourteen

August had never been surrounded by so many people in his life.

Obviously that was a lie. He'd been around a whole lot more people than the current company, but because he only had eyes for one woman, the "everyone else" seemed superfluous.

Too much.

"What do you think of Dan?" Tanya whispered from his side. "Do you think he's fitting in?"

"I don't know." August looked over at the guy who was just returning from his third or fourth trip to the bathroom. "He's sure skipping out of here a lot."

"I think the singing waiters are driving him a little crazy."

The singing waiters drove everyone over eight years old crazy. But that was a given. August didn't have much patience for a guy who made his feelings so transparently known. "He seems kind of a wuss. Have you been dating him long?"

Tanya blew out a laugh. "No. This is our second date."

August watched as Dan rubbed his temples when a giant crab started singing near a fountain to their left, then he chuckled. "You'll be lucky if you have a third. I think you've scared him. Rockin' Roberts isn't for the weak."

Tanya looked at her date sympathetically. "I know, but I figured trial by fire and all that."

August laughed and tried to catch Evie's attention, but she was arguing over the children's menu with Jenna. Apparently, Jenna no longer wanted to eat from the place mat menu, and wanted what the big people ate. Of course, she didn't like any of the big people's selections and wouldn't listen to anyone's obvious lies about what was on it.

At the other end of their table, August heard his mom telling Mike and Jan all about Harmonious Haven and Dr. Wayne and her date with him to the movies. The very thought of her dating still gave him the willies.

Luckily, his current eating partner was small, picky and darn cute. "Missy, how are those goldfish?" he asked, pressing his nose to her neck and making her giggle.

Bright blue eyes met his with a snaggle-toothed smile. "Fish."

"I'm thinking of having fish, too. What do you think? Catfish or grouper?"

"Fffff-fish," Missy pronounced with an ebullient kick of her feet.

"Good choice."

Missy giggled and held out her hands, which August now knew meant she wanted to be held. Easily swinging her out of her high chair, August fitted her on his lap.

As expected, she molded to him like a starfish, treating him once again to a beautiful smile.

What he hadn't expected was everyone's reaction.

"You're holding a baby," Tanya pointed out, her eyes lighting up.

"You never were the sharpest tool in the shed. Watch out, Dan. She's a real live wire."

"Shut up." Tanya looked around the table for support. "All I'm saying is that this is a new thing. You look really comfortable holding Missy, August. Almost like you're ready to be a parent."

Oh, for Pete's sake. "Tanya, worry about yourself."

"I'd rather worry about you."

Luckily, Jan came to his rescue. "Missy's always been the easiest baby in the world. She likes you, too."

"Wasn't I easy?" Jenna asked.

Mike looked straight at his eldest granddaughter. "No."

Everyone laughed, even Jenna, who was so stunned by her grandpa's bluntness, she was momentarily speechless.

"If you hold Missy now, we'll never get her back in the high chair tonight," Evie warned.

"I kind of figured that," August said as Missy reached for the pile of goldfish he'd transferred to his plate, contemplated them all very seriously, then popped one in her mouth. "But that's okay. I like holding her."

"She is a dear," Jan said with a smile.

Conversation moved on, and August did his best to concentrate on all kinds of things he suddenly didn't care about.

Tanya's date with the wuss. His mother's bridge club and the fund-raiser for the arts. Wayne's trouble with the two par fives at the golf club.

All he saw and heard was Evie. He liked the way she was patient with Jenna and truly interested in Beverly. How she laughed when the ancient animated animals started singing "In the Jungle" and smiled at him when Missy got scared and burst into tears.

In fact, all he wanted to do was pull Evie into his arms and maybe even hold her like he was holding Missy.

Except he'd be smelling her perfume.

Breathing in her scent.

Feeling the way her body felt, slim and strong…yet feminine. And then, it would be so easy to kiss her.

Slip off that bright pink sundress she was wearing and—

"You okay, there, August? Our server's been asking if you wanted another Coors for a good minute."

"I'm fine, sorry. I guess my mind just got away from me."

"It got somewhere," Tanya murmured under her breath.

He was having completely inappropriate fantasies at a family restaurant with dancing lobsters and a baby on his lap.

But he wasn't too old to kick his sister on the shin.

She rubbed her leg. "Ouch!"

Dan tried to come to the rescue. "What happened?"

Tanya just smiled. "Everything. Everything happened. And isn't that just the best news in the world?"

Evie met his glance then. "You okay?"

No, no he was not. He'd just realized he'd fallen in love with Evie Ray all over again and that it was completely one-sided. "Yeah, sure."

"Dinner's fun."

"It's a blast."

"Would you like to go for a walk later?" Her voice was full of promise.

If they did that, he'd pull her into his arms and kiss her again. Maybe go find a secluded cove and do a whole lot more than that. Struggling to keep his voice calm, he nodded. "I'd like that."

"Good."

Tanya winked and barely hid a laugh from behind her napkin.

August wasn't proud, but he did the only thing any self-respecting brother could do...he kicked his sister one more time.

Chapter Fifteen

"I need to talk to you," Evie told Tanya as she followed her friend down the narrow hallway to the main dance classroom.

Tanya, dressed in a slate-blue leotard, pink tights and some kind of flowing black wraparound skirt, glanced over her shoulder and frowned. "Now's not a good time. I'm working."

"You haven't returned my phone calls."

"Evie, you only left one message, and it was around ten last night."

"You're right, but I really do need some advice."

Tanya looked as if she was fighting a smile as she moved to the far end of the room and started pulling out portable ballet bars. "I'd love to help you, but I can't. I've got a class of eleven-year-olds in five minutes."

"What about after class?" Evie mentally ran through her day, and realized she probably had another two hours before her parents would pick up that glazed look they got after an afternoon at the baby pool.

"No can do. I've got an adult strength and toning class next."

"Oh. All right, then," she replied.

She was about to leave when Tanya touched her hand. "You really need to talk right now, don't you?"

"Yeah."

Tanya stared at her for a full minute, then pointed to her office. "Go have a seat. I'm going to go ask Melissa to lead the warm-ups today."

"Are you sure?"

"Positive. The girls won't mind." In no time at all, Tanya sat down across from her. "I've got about fifteen minutes."

Evie didn't waste time. "Tell me what August has said to you about me. Does he like me?"

"You know he does."

"I don't know how much."

"Evie, you need to grow up and ask him. We aren't in junior high anymore."

Thinking of her response to August's kisses, Evie scowled. "My hormones are so messed up, I might as well be. Come on Tanya, what did he say?"

"Not much. We don't talk about crushes during late night bowls of ice cream."

"Tanya, I wouldn't have called you, come over here and made you sit here if I didn't seriously need your help."

"I'm sorry." As the front door chimed, Tanya motioned to Melissa through the glass, then shut her office door. "Here's the deal. August likes you. He's always liked you, but he's afraid that once again, you're not serious."

Once again? A sinking feeling settled in. "I'm serious."

"How serious?"

"How serious does he want me to be? He's got to realize that I'm only here for another two weeks. Then, I'll be back in Texas and he'll be here."

Tanya's eyes betrayed her disappointment. "So that's

how it is? You're just going to come to Bishop's Gate, break my brother's heart, then leave. Again?"

"Excuse me—I have a life in Grapevine." What did Tanya think she was going to do? Drop everything and move in with her parents?

"He's got a life here that you're messing with. Evie, I can't believe you encouraged something you didn't have any intention of finishing."

"I never said that."

"It sounds like it."

"Then you haven't been listening to me," Evie fired back, hurt that Tanya was putting her whole life into such simplistic terms. "I can't just pick up and change all my priorities for a summer romance. I have children."

Tanya stretched out her legs in front of her with a sigh. "That's why I didn't want to talk about this. Not in a five-minute phone conversation. Not in between dance classes. But you have no patience."

"I have patience. I just wanted your opinion."

Tanya's lips curved upward. "Now."

"All right. Yeah, now." Tapping her foot, her grumbled, "I suck at patience."

"You sure do."

"I just wanted to know what you thought August was thinking."

"I think he's glad you're in his life, but remembers how you cut off the relationship in a snap that summer before college."

A strong sense of foreboding slipped in the room. "What are you talking about?"

"I'm talking about a certain baby that almost was."

"I can't believe August told you."

"I can't believe you thought he'd never tell a soul."

Evie hadn't. When she'd realized that she wasn't

pregnant, she'd jumped headfirst into a new life, doing her best to make everything right. "I'm sorry. It never occurred to me that he would have talked about that time."

"Ouch." Tanya's eyes, so like August's, filled with hurt. "Listen to us, arguing over things that are over and done with. That's why I didn't want to do this at all. It's not my problem that you don't want to commit, but you can't fault me for coming to my brother's side."

The stark words urged Evie to be completely honest, too. "Tanya, I'm afraid August will lose interest in me one day, just like John did. I'm afraid that one day I'm going to be making dinner plans while he's calling lawyers."

Tanya stood up, checked her hair in the small mirror, then walked to the door. "Don't you see that he's afraid of the same thing, Evie? John may have left you…but to August, you did the same damn thing." When Melissa knocked on the window, Tanya smoothed back her hair and opened her door. "I've got to go."

"Thanks, T."

She paused. "For what?"

"For being a good enough friend to be honest."

Tanya reached out and squeezed her hand. "One day, do the same thing for me."

As Tanya entered the classroom, Evie slowly walked out the door, thinking about how things used to be…and how they never were.

Chapter Sixteen

When she got home, August was waiting for her. For a split second, she caught a glimpse of what her future could be.

He was sitting on the red-and-yellow rug, playing with blocks with Missy, saying *gato* with Dora on TV and helping Jenna with her pile of Legos.

He looked relaxed and happy and not a bit out of place. Almost as comfortable as John, but different, because when she entered the room, August looked really happy to see her.

Had John ever looked at her that way? Like she was pecan pie and that first cup of coffee in the morning, all wrapped up into one?

"Hi. Where've you been?"

After kissing Missy and Jenna on the tops of their heads, she sat down on the ground and joined them. "I was actually at Tanya's dance studio."

"Doing what?"

She did her best eleven-year-old imitation. "Dancing?"

As she hoped, August laughed. "I'm going to ask again. Why?"

"I needed some advice," she admitted. She didn't want

to lie or to gloss over her jumbled emotions. "I don't know what's going on between us."

He scooted a little closer. Luckily, Dora had done her usual hypnotizing to Jenna, so she wasn't paying any attention to the grown-up conversation. "Why did you ask Tanya? I could have told you."

"I realized soon after I arrived that I'd made a serious lapse in judgment. She pretty much said the same thing."

August took her hand. And as his fingers linked through hers, she realized that he was always doing that. Touching her, making her feel wanted. Better. Attractive.

She loved his attention.

"I think what's happening is we're finally acting on what started between us all those years ago," he said softly.

Evie still stared at their linked hands. "And that is…?"

"Are you going to make me say it? Are you going to make me do everything, Evie?"

Was that what she was doing? "I don't want to."

"Then say what I want to hear."

"All I know is that I like being with you."

"So far, so good."

Feeling braver, she admitted, "I like the way you make me feel."

"You make me feel good, too."

"I feel comfortable with you, and you make me feel like everything in my crazy, mixed-up life is going to work out."

He raised their linked hands and kissed where their fingers joined. "So there's no problem."

"There's a big problem. Its name is Texas."

"You could move here. It's where you want to be, anyway."

That was the exact wrong thing for him to say. "I can't."

"Sure you can."

"There's John." She whispered his name. Afraid to say it louder, just in case Jenna heard.

"He's not your husband. Not any longer."

"He plays a huge role in my life. He always will. I can't move away from him."

"I have a resort here, Evie. It's my dad's legacy. I can't leave it."

"I'm not asking you to. Just like I don't think you should start asking me for things I can't do."

Quietly he said, "You aren't going to budge, are you?"

Standing up, Evie pulled August over to the kitchen. "What if things were reversed? Would you want your ex-wife to take your kids from you? Move them three states away because she suddenly decided she was in love?"

He didn't hesitate. "No."

"Then don't ask that of me."

"What can I ask you to do?" he murmured, looking directly at her, giving her no time to say anything but what was in her heart.

She took a deep breath and made the plunge. "If you want to try and make things work, long distance, I'm willing to try."

Relief filled his gaze. "You mean that, don't you?"

"Of course I do. I'm not saying no to you, August. I'm just saying no to moving to Bishop's Gate. And I care enough about you to not ask you to move for me." As soon as the words left her mouth, Evie held her breath. This was the first step forward she'd made in the relationship department since her divorce.

Actually, it was the only step forward she'd made, the only step forward that counted, and it was sending her into a grip of panic, of uncertainty. Like she was balancing on a tight rope over a deep, dark ravine.

Had she just made another mistake and was about to free-fall into an abyss?

His green eyes searched hers. Time seemed to stand still as he looked her over again, gazing at her, making her feel as if she was worth a sacrifice. Worth his time, worth living apart.

Worth more than she ever remembered being willing to feel.

"Okay."

"Okay? You're okay?"

And then no words were spoken, because he kissed her. Tenderly, his lips brushed hers, coaxing her to relax, coaxing her mouth open, deepening the kiss, touching her tongue with his.

Right there in the kitchen. After pulling her farther in away from the girls' line of vision, August ran his hands along her back, cupped her bottom, nudged her closer. His thighs parted, and she stepped in, filling the gap, remembering how it felt to be even closer to him. It was like a dream and the most amazing discovery in the world. Tension built in her, tension she'd all but forgotten.

That she'd wondered if she could ever feel again. With tenderness, she held his face in her palms and kissed him wholeheartedly.

"Whoa!" her dad said, as he entered the kitchen.

Out of breath, Evie stepped back. "Sorry, Daddy. Me and August, we're, uh…"

"I have a pretty good idea what I saw, sunshine. I don't need the play-by-play."

"We were celebrating."

Mike folded his arms across his chest as he looked around the kitchen. "That we have bread in the pantry?"

"That we're officially a couple."

Confusion gave way to sheer enthusiasm. "Yeah?"

"Yeah."

Mike called out to the laundry room. "Jan, get in here." Turning to Evie, he said, "Don't move. Your mother's going to want to hear this."

"Hear what?" Jan asked.

"Evie finally came to her senses. She and August are going to get married."

Whoa, there. "Not married. We're…" She looked at August and hoped he could think, because at the moment, all words escaped her.

Once again, he didn't disappoint. "We're going steady."

"But in a good way," Evie finished triumphantly.

When her dad looked like he was about to start spouting off a bunch of new ideas, her mom cut him off. "I think that's great. We'll just see how things go from here, right?"

"Right."

"Momma? Missy pooped!"

Jenna's proclamation made everything seem just right. That was what life was, anyway. There were no guarantees. Just hopes and maybes.

Spilled toys and dirty diapers.

Her mom frowned. "I'll go take—"

"No, Mom. That's a mommy duty, not a grandma one. August, will you be still here when I get back?"

"I was here before you came home," he said with a smile. "I'm not going anywhere."

Evie couldn't help smiling as she joined Jenna and a smelly Missy in the family room. "Thanks for letting me know about Missy, Jenna."

"Welcome."

"Come here, princess," Evie murmured to Missy, who was wearing a very disgruntled expression. "Let's get you cleaned up."

And as she took Missy downstairs, Evie couldn't believe that she was looking toward the future again. Some things were almost too good to be true.

Chapter Seventeen

What was happening was never what August wanted. What he'd wanted, back when he dreamed of Evie late at night and imagined that they'd have a life together, was that she would decide she hated Texas and couldn't wait to move to Florida.

His fantasies had involved her having no goals besides ones that were intertwined with his.

In high school, back when he'd been trying to drum up the courage to beg her to transfer schools, he'd imagined himself running Silver Shells with his dad, and coming home to a tiny cottage with Evie. He'd never imagined having to do much except want her. Love her. But now things were different.

Because deep down, he still had planned on Evie giving up her house, her friends, her life, her daughter's schools and friends and comforts, and moving everything to Florida because it was where he needed to be. How selfish could he be?

And, Lord help him, he'd been caught off guard by her honesty.

It had only been after her stark candor, and her suggestion that he try to imagine an ex-wife pulling his children away from him, that he conceded that maybe—just maybe—things weren't going to work out like he'd planned.

But now these ten years had brought about a change. Before, when Evie had been so relieved about the negative pregnancy test, he'd felt strangely let down.

When she'd stopped writing him because she'd been dating John, he'd said okay. He'd never even thought about transferring to Texas, or flying out to be with her. To make her see that things could be different. To see that they were worth too much to just give them up so easily.

He'd always regretted the fact that he'd let her go without a fight.

Now, after almost doing the same thing again, he was willing to compromise.

But what, actually, was he willing to do?

To clear his mind, he did what he always did—he put on his trunks, grabbed a towel and a bottle of water and headed to the beach.

The day was hot and clear—no different than any other day the past week. But the sand was like hot coals under his feet and the air felt like it was stuck in a vacuum. Not a bit of breeze floated around him.

August almost welcomed the heat and the saunalike conditions. As sweat poured down his back, he stretched, then walked into the surf, wading out, welcoming the sharp sting of the cool water meeting his body. Finally, after pulling his goggles over his eyes, August took a deep breath, pushed forward with his feet and began to swim.

Swimming in the ocean was hard. The salt stung his cheeks, the water tasted tart against his lips. The currents fought against his every move. But August didn't truly enjoy swimming anywhere else.

Using a freestyle stroke, he propelled himself forward, and let his muscles take over.

After forty minutes, he waded back to the beach, shook out his towel and lay on his back, exhausted.

Around him, kids ran and jumped, spraying a light mist of sand across his body. August welcomed the sprinkling—it was as familiar to him as hearing the surf when he closed his eyes. As having po'boys on Sunday afternoons and watching the fireworks over the pier on holidays, and as familiar as his dad's office chair was.

And knowing his mom was nearby.

How could he give all of that up?

Any of it up?

A shadow fell over him. When he peeked out, he spied Tanya standing just to his left, wearing khaki shorts and a Silver Shells T-shirt.

"There you are. I've been looking for you everywhere."

Raising himself to rest on his elbows, he squinted in her direction. "Is anything wrong?"

"Yes, as a matter of fact. The toilet in the Marlin cottage is stopped up and I can't get ahold of Bruce."

"Great. Okay, I'll get up."

"Listen, I think we need to hire Bruce full-time."

There was so much force in his sister's voice, August sat up and decided he needed to really listen. "What brought this on?"

"A lot of things."

"Such as?"

"Bruce is really handy, and it drives me crazy having to page him and wonder if he's close by or not. We need him on the payroll. It would free up a lot of time for both of us."

"I agree, but having Bruce on payroll would seriously change our finances."

"I was thinking about that, but I'm not so sure. I think we need to meet with the accountant again."

August pulled up his towel, shook it out and started walking back to the resort next to his sister. "May I ask why?"

"I'd like to do more. More around here."

There was no way August was going to let her work 24/7. "Tanya, you already have a job. I know the dance studio keeps you busy. When were you planning to work at the resort? In the middle of the night?"

She didn't laugh at his joke. "That's something I've been meaning to speak with you about. I do like the dance studio, but I think it's run its course. I'm ready to do something different. I've been thinking I'd like to do something less confining."

"Less confining? Tanya, I've only been out of the office for two hours and we're having a minor emergency."

"It's only an emergency because we don't have Bruce on staff."

"We don't have Bruce on staff because we can't afford to." He looked at her sideways. "And what about the dance studio?"

"August, if I stop working at the dance studio, I can sell it. That money can go to the resort and my salary."

"But we won't need both of us working here full-time."

"We might if you start going to Texas a lot."

August stopped in his tracks. "I never said I was going to do that. And you can't sell Mom's studio. She's planned on you managing it. If you sold it, it would break her heart."

"But no one ever asked me if that was what I wanted, August."

Slowly, he sat down on the cement curb. "I've never heard you speak of all of this before. Where did it come from?"

"I don't know. Evie, I guess."

"Evie?"

"We've gotten closer over the last few weeks. Close enough to make me realize that she and I aren't too different. Both of us jumped in to things because we thought we were doing the right things, but instead, all we were doing was setting ourselves up for disappointment."

All of this was news to him. "That's how the dance studio was for you?"

"I tried to love it, but I don't. I love to *dance,* August. But I don't love teaching."

"What are you going to tell Mom?"

She looked down at her feet before meeting his gaze. "I'm going to tell her that it's time for me to move on, like she has. It's time to do what I want, not just what I *thought* I should want to do. I like working at Silver Shells, August."

"You do a good job."

Hope shined in her face. "Really?"

"Really." To his surprise, August realized he wasn't lying. Tanya did do a great job with the resort. She got along well with their guests and was far more organized than he was. She also worked hard on the resort's Web site and was responsible for a lot of their new visitors.

How come he was just now realizing that?

"See, if I'm here, you'll be able to see Evie more," Tanya said. "You'll be able to visit her in Texas. Get to spend more time with her and the girls."

"You've got a good point."

Tanya smiled. "You might really enjoy being in Texas more."

"Maybe." He would feel easier leaving the resort if it was in Tanya's capable hands.

"Yep. The only thing you won't have is the sand and ocean."

The coast of Florida felt as much a part of him as his limbs. August couldn't imagine going months without hearing the surf or looking out into the gulf water in the early morning. But, perhaps he'd find other scenic views? Ones that involved city skylines and the broad Texas skies Evie was so fond of? "I'll just have to make sure Evie comes this way as often as possible."

"She will, August, I'm sure of it," Tanya said confidently. "I think right now she'll be willing to do whatever it takes to make things work between you."

August hoped so. After all these years, he couldn't bear to think what would happen to his heart if she didn't.

EVIE FLIPPED BACK A wayward strand of hair and tried not to think about John glaring at her through the phone. "I have not been remiss, John. I signed Jenna up for soccer weeks before we left for Florida."

"But practice starts this week."

Evie winced at the whine in her ex-husband's voice and tried to see through her frustration with him to the real problem—he wanted to see his girls. With almost the last bit of patience she had, Evie said slowly, "I already spoke to the coach and she understands this is a special circumstance."

"Special circumstance? You've pulled Jenna away from her entire life."

"The last time I checked, her sister, mother and grandparents were part of her life, too," she said, finally letting her anger fly. Patience was way overrated.

"You know what I'm talking about. The Cyclones will already be a cohesive unit by the time she returns. Jenna won't have any idea what to do."

Now he was getting ridiculous. "Have you met our daughter? She's tall, gangly, has red curly hair and was born knowing everything? She's never *not* known what she wants to do. Jenna's going to march out on that field and tell the team where to stand."

To her surprise and relief, John chuckled. "Point taken. Still, she needs to practice."

"I know she does," Evie said, tempering her tone. "I brought her soccer ball and she's been practicing here."

"With who? August?"

Well, that came out of left field. "How did you know about him?"

"Jenna the Informer." Amusement teased his voice as he admitted, "She drew me a picture of him. I got it in her last batch of pictures."

Evie was surprised. "Yeah?"

"Yeah. He looks like a badass. He's purple and has a really big head."

In spite of herself, Evie laughed. Their conversation was vintage John. He'd get irritated, then get over it just as quickly.

And that humor made her see things from his side, though it was the last place she wanted to view the world. At the moment, John had gone twenty-one days without seeing the girls. If the situation had been reversed, Evie knew she'd be contemplating flying to Florida just to get a hug.

"How about we leave four days early? That puts us back in Grapevine next Thursday."

After a pause, he said, "You're okay with that?"

No, she wasn't. But it was time to get back to reality and her responsibilities. Just because she didn't want to face obligations didn't mean the girls had to suffer. "I'll be okay. If we get back early, I'll have a chance to get school supplies and get organized."

"If you get them back early, how about I do that for you?"

"You'd do that?"

"Ev, I can go to Wal-Mart as easy as you can."

"There is the back-to-school outfit."

"Well, I can't handle that one. I'm sure Jenna will hate everything I pick out."

"Maybe not, John." Since he'd already brought August into the conversation, Evie pulled up Terri, too. "Maybe Terri could choose something."

"Maybe, but I'm not sure if Terri's ready for that one. Remember, I've lived with our little general, too."

Evie laughed.

"How about I take Missy and Jenna from Friday to Sunday? You can spend that time recovering from the trip." Compromise. That was what all good mothers did, right? After pulling out the calendar from her purse, she nodded. She'd still have Labor Day home with the girls. "That will work."

"Thanks, Evie. I've been going crazy, missing them."

Tears pricked her eyes because she knew John wasn't stretching the truth at all. He loved their girls as much as she did. One thing she would always admire about him was the fact that he'd never tried to hide his love for them, or shirk his responsibilities. "You're welcome."

After she hung up, Evie looked at the calendar again. She had four more days in Florida and then it was time to go home.

Already she had a feeling that the hot sun in Grapevine wouldn't hold a candle to Bishop's Gate. With a sigh, she stood up and slowly climbed the stairs to tell her parents.

It wasn't an exaggeration to say that she was braced for the worst.

Chapter Eighteen

As expected, her dad was the most vocal. "That damn John. I knew he was going to pull something like this. Can't he manage to think of you for once?"

Luckily, they were sitting on the back porch, away from the sleeping girls. "Lower your voice, Dad. The whole resort is going to hear you."

"So?"

"I don't have a desire for them to hear my business. Plus, if they can hear you, so will the girls. If you wake them up with your carrying on, I'm going to make you rock Missy back to sleep."

Mike rubbed a hand across his forehead. "Sorry. But damn it to hell, Evie, you shouldn't have caved in."

Evie didn't dare look at her mother. From the moment she'd told them about the switch in travel plans, Evie had felt like she was a teenager, going against their united front. "I didn't cave in," she protested. "I simply attempted to understand his point of view."

"It would be nice if he did that for you sometimes."

"He's the one who suggested I come down here."

Her dad's temper exploded. "Because he wasn't going to be at home in the first place!"

"Mike, you're not helping," her mother said softly as she stood up and closed the glass door that led into the house.

Evie gulped. Over the years, she couldn't remember a time the door was shut except during natural disasters. The fact that the door was needed to silence out-of-control tempers made her wish she could go slink into some hole.

"Why you take his side all the time, I don't know," her dad continued, this time far more quietly. "He's made you miserable, Evie."

"Actually, I've been doing a pretty good job of that all on my own. Besides, I'm not miserable right now. I'm happy." As a matter of fact, she was happier than she'd been in some time. "Well, I was happy until you started freaking out."

After looking at Jan, her father patted the chair next to him. "Move to Florida."

"I can't do that," Evie said, though she did move to sit by his side.

"You *won't*. You should, though. You're in that dead-end job."

"It's a good job, and I like who I work for."

"You're stuck in Grapevine, even though you've always been happiest here."

"I've liked Grapevine just fine, Daddy."

Mike frowned. "Then, of course, there's the—"

Evie had had enough. She was tired of everyone telling her she looked bad, she was too tired, that she needed to do more for herself. "We already talked about this. Several times."

"Obviously not enough." Resting his elbows on his knees, he said, "Let's just think about how we can make this work."

"Let's not." Standing up, she said, "I'm going to bed. I can't go through two tough conversations in one day."

"Sit down, Evelyn," her mother said. "Your dramatics aren't helping anything." Before Evie could point out that she was not the one with the problem, her mother turned to her dad and put an evil eye on him, too. "And you, Michael, pipe down. Our daughter is not moving to Siberia, she's being an adult."

Evie sat, catching her dad's mouthed "Siberia?", and shrugged.

Already the tension on the back porch eased up.

"Evie, I think you're doing the right thing," her mother finally said.

Evie turned to her in surprise. "You do?"

"I do. A good mother has to put her children first. That's all there is to it. And you, my dear, have always done that." After a brief look at Mike, her mother leaned forward and spoke again. "Now, I just have one more question. What are you going to do about August?"

"We're going to work things out."

"What do you think he's going to say when you tell him you're leaving early?"

"I don't know," Evie admitted. "I hope he'll understand that I'm doing what I feel I have to do. I'm hoping you both will understand that, too."

Very softly, her mother said, "We understand you're a grown woman with a lot on her shoulders…who's handling things exceptionally well."

Her dad squeezed her hand. "Missy and Jenna are wonderful girls, sweetheart," he said, finally giving in. "You really are a good mom."

Hearing those words from the two people she admired most meant the world to her. Swallowing a lump in her throat, she whispered, "Thank you."

"You're welcome, sunshine."

Jan moved closer. "August loves you, Evie. I'm sure of it."

"I…care for him, too. We'll work things out."

Her dad leaned back in his chair. "But if you did want to move here, it would sure be nice."

"John can't move jobs, Dad. And I'm not going to move the girls from him because I've fallen in love with someone in Florida. Plus, John's family is there…the girls are used to seeing their other grandparents on a regular basis."

"You've fallen in love, Evie?"

Oh, for goodness' sake, she had. "I guess I have," she said, feeling like once again her life was spinning out of control. "My life is a mess."

Jan smiled. "No, my dear, I think your life is finally right."

For once Evie wished she had something smart to say because, as if on cue, August came strolling up the flagstones from the trail on the beach. "Hi, Rays. I saw your lights on and thought I'd stop by to say hello. Is that okay?"

Her dad stood up quickly. "It's fine. Want a beer?"

August turned to her, his expression full of concern. "No, thanks."

Evie realized she hadn't done a very good job of hiding her emotions.

"Come have a seat, August," her dad said. "Jan and I were just heading on inside. I bet Evie could use some company."

Still August hesitated. "Okay?"

She nodded imperceptibly as her parents gave more excuses and left them.

With easy motions, he opened the outside screen door

as her parents opened the glass and inside screen and quickly left them.

Then, all Evie was aware of was August, and his smile that was completely, obviously, just for her. After pressing a kiss to her brow, he murmured, "You want to go sit in our spot?"

"Definitely," she said, stepping toward him as if she was in a trance. Next, it was only the perfect thing to do to take his hand.

But instead of walking toward their familiar iron chairs, August pulled her away from the lights surrounding the house, into the shadows of the hydrangea bushes. Pulled her closer.

And finally, Evie stepped into his arms like she'd been counting the minutes.

Maybe she had.

Now her heart was bursting with need for him, and the need to pour out all the truths. She didn't want to leave him. She couldn't wait to go to bed with him. For the first time in a very long time, she felt whole.

But now, all that really mattered was that he was kissing her in a way that made her feel like she was wanted and special.

"God, I love kissing you," he murmured, wrapping his arms around her waist and holding her close. "I guess I wasn't too subtle about why I came over here, was I?"

"There was no need to be." Unable to keep from lightening the moment, she added, "We both know I'm irresistible."

"You are that," he said, right before claiming her mouth again.

Oh, he tasted good. He felt good. Like August. Like mint and warmth, and everything good. Like honesty and the ocean all mixed up together. And no one had ever kissed her the way he did. As if there was nowhere on the entire earth he'd rather be.

Somehow they stumbled to the grass in the shelter of some low-lying palms. Somehow they sank to the ground. Well, August did. Evie found herself sprawled across his lap, enjoying being cradled in his arms before curving her hips to cuddle closer, just as his hand caressed her thighs. Then snaked upward and cupped her breast as they deepened the kiss once again.

It had been a long time since she'd felt attractive. Desirable. August made her feel all those things.

After waiting a split second, August deftly slid her tank top from her shoulders, revealing a terribly skimpy bright pink bra.

August smiled briefly before shoving down those straps, too.

And then all of a sudden, life stood still. No longer was she a mother of two with mountains of responsibilities and stacks of bills and doubts.

No longer did she wish her arms were better-toned, her hair better-conditioned, her breasts bigger than a barely there A cup.

She no longer cared about stretch marks and a stomach that, while flat, sure didn't look bikini-ready.

All of a sudden, she was seventeen and in August's arms again. And yet, something was different. Maybe it was experience and knowledge. Maybe it was the fact that she now analyzed things instead of just feeling. But no matter what, she knew the truth.

What she felt was love, and it felt fresh and pure and as in her grasp as anything she'd ever felt before.

"I love you, August," she breathed.

Stiffening, August broke away. For a split second, he stared at her, out of breath. Evie was sure she'd just said the absolute worst thing in the world. Had she just alienated him, too?

Had she just imagined he'd been feeling the same things she was? Despair flooded her before she had the nerve to meet his eyes.

And then, as she caught his pleasure in those gorgeous green irises, Evie knew that for the first time, everything was totally, completely right.

He loved her, too. "You sure?"

"I'm sure," she said, happy in the comfort of his arms, so happy she didn't even care that she was almost thirty and sitting topless in the night air.

"I love you, too," he whispered, then to her surprise, gently slid her bra and tank top back into place.

As his hands rubbed over her aroused skin, a sense of panic engulfed her. "What are you doing?"

"Covering you up. What I want to do right now should probably be done inside. Want to go to my place?"

She did. But she didn't want to take things further until she told him her news. "I do, but I need to tell you something first."

His eyes softened. Rubbing the back of his hand across her jaw, he said, "What? You love my body?"

In spite of her churning nerves, she laughed. "I do love your body, but a woman would have to be blind not to. You're perfect."

He was enough of a man to look extremely pleased with that remark. "Ready to see all my perfection?"

"In a minute."

His gaze turned serious. "Are you worried about protection? Because I have—"

She covered his lips with her fingers. "I'm not worried about that, but, ah, thank you."

"Then?"

"I have to tell you something." She scrambled off his lap and sat next to him, putting some much-needed space between them.

He reached for her, obviously wanting to keep them close. "What do you need to tell me? That you've been wanting me for years?"

She shifted just as he leaned forward to brush his lips against her neck. Thank goodness he didn't make contact. It would have been all too obvious that August—and his kisses—affected her like nothing else in the world.

Well, at least nothing that she knew of yet. "This is important."

Slowly he leaned back. In the dim glow of the solar garden lights artfully planted nearby, Evie could barely make out the slight change in his demeanor. All teasing was gone, and its place was wariness. "Okay."

"I talked to John, and we've decided that I'm going to go back four days early." Evie held her breath, wondering how he was going to react. So far, she and August hadn't had the opportunity to get into much of an argument…at least not one that mattered.

But right then, at that minute, Evie had to admit that his opinion and his reaction mattered a lot. She didn't want to disappoint him, didn't want to have to spend the next twenty minutes defending John. She just wanted—no, *needed*—him to understand that she was a single mom trying to do the best she could.

"So, you'll be leaving on Wednesday?"

There was no going back, although right that very minute, she wanted nothing more than to pretend that she didn't have a single thing to worry about other than what August would think of the changes in her body after all these years. "Right."

"Why?"

"John misses the girls terribly," she said, though there were a dozen excuses she could have said. "He asked me if I'd come back so he could spend a weekend with them before school started. I couldn't say no."

August stared at her a good, long moment, then nodded. "That makes sense."

His reaction was so opposite to what she'd expected she was caught off-kilter. "It does?"

"What, you don't want me to be understanding?"

"Truthfully, I wasn't sure what you were going to say. My parents weren't very understanding."

"What did Jenna say?"

Jenna. Leave it to August to remember who was going to be the most affected by the news. "I haven't told her yet, but I think she's going to be thrilled."

"I heard her crying for him the other night."

"Jenna always cries for whoever isn't there. John and I learned to ignore that."

"But it's been a while."

Evie looked at her hands. "I know you think he and I could have done things differently...and I bet we could have. But the thing with John is that I know without a doubt that he loves those girls. When he told me that it had been twenty-one days since he'd seen them, I knew I didn't have a choice." Hesitantly, she said, "If our situations had been reversed, I would have been counting, too."

August turned away for a moment, his body lean and fluid, yet slightly tense. "Evie, I understand your need to go back early. I also—Lord, help me—understand John's desire to see his daughters. So, I'm okay with all of that."

"I'm surprised."

He flashed a smile. "In a way, I'm surprised at myself, too. So, what about us? When can I see you again?"

Evie felt as though a giant lump had just been lodged in her throat. She struggled to find the words to reply to him.

Because truthfully, she didn't know what to say.

Chapter Nineteen

When Evie practically started choking to death instead of answering him right away, August knew that there was more at work than just busy schedules. Mentally, he cursed himself. There was a significant portion of his body that had digressed in age during the last twenty minutes.

At the moment, what he really wanted to do was get into Evie Ray's pants.

He wasn't proud of that fact. He doubted he would ever admit it, but it was the simple truth. Just minutes ago, he'd been in heaven. He'd dreamed about their time together at Cascade Cove over the years until he was sure it played as clearly in his mind as if he had a video of their time together sitting next to his bed.

The fact that he was once again going to feel her next to him was a heady thought.

"I don't know when. I've got to get the girls settled, then there's work..." She finally said. "I know I don't want to lose you."

He wasn't about to lose her, either. "Invite me. Invite me to come see you."

"You'd do that?"

"At the moment, I'm pretty damn sure I'd follow you to the moon."

She giggled. Childish and full of life, it warmed his heart. "August, please come to Grapevine and visit."

He linked his fingers through hers and tugged gently. "Visit soon?"

She slid back toward him without a bit of resistance. "Soon." Eyes widening, she said, "John is going to have the girls over Labor Day. I know it's just days from when I leave here…but, if you wanted…you could come then."

"You'll be ready for me then?"

Her eyes darkened, just the way they used to when she was aroused. "I'm ready for you now."

"Good. Then it's settled. I'm coming to Dallas to see you over Labor Day weekend." He pulled her up. "Is there anything else that you have to discuss?"

She shook her head as she let him lead her away from the cottage, down the path, toward his own place.

"No more important things to tell me about?"

"My mind's practically empty at the moment."

They were almost running. August knew he was being ridiculous. Knew there was really no hurry.

Knew he was finally getting what he wanted—Evie in his arms, Evie's love—but he still couldn't wait. When they got to his street, he guided her to his own cottage, laughing when she tripped on her sandals, then finally ended up taking them off and carrying them in her hands.

"I can't believe I haven't been over here yet," she said as they walked through his back door.

His place wasn't the showstopper her parents' was, but it did have a lot of personal touches. Direct TV had come out and installed an HDTV receiver to go with his forty-two-inch plasma. A state-of-the-art stereo system was wired throughout, so he could hear either Mozart or the Talking Heads or ESPN in every room of the house.

The décor had never really mattered too much to him, except that it had to be comfortable. Tanya had decorated the whole place in tans and blues, making it seem like the ocean had paid a visit to his place and left its mark. Even the huge model ship that rested in the landing was reminiscent of the sea.

Evie strode right over to it. "August, this is beautiful!"

"Thanks. It's supposed to be a model of the first America's Cup ship."

Her eyes widened. "Did you build this?"

"No," he said, amused. "I bought it at an auction a couple of months after my dad died. He was the ship builder."

When she acted like she was going to bend down and inspect the thing, August easily picked her up. As he'd half expected, she squealed. "What are you doing?"

"I'm getting you back on track," he murmured, carrying her into his bedroom. After depositing her on the bed, he said, "Now, do I have to give you a tour of this room, or will you stay focused?"

She gave him a once-over, a slow enough examination to make him think that for once in his life, he'd done a very, very good thing by taking complete control.

"I'll stay focused," she murmured.

"Good," he said, then climbed onto his big king-size bed next to her and kissed her again.

And then, nothing else seemed to matter, because she was in his arms. Just like she used to be. And it was just like he'd dreamed…and yet it was different. Better.

Once again, he brushed back the straps of her knit top, pulled it away from her skin and enjoyed the sight of Evie in bright pink.

This time, Evie didn't look embarrassed in the slightest. He was glad because he'd always thought she was exquisitely pretty. After kissing her breasts through the shiny satin, he gave in to temptation and unclasped the garment.

And then there was only Evie in his arms. "Pretty," he murmured, just before kissing every place where there used to be fabric. Evie arched her back, letting him know how much she desired him, and shifting so their bodies were even closer.

Then there was the simple task of removing the rest of their clothes. Getting to know each newly bared spot up close and personal. Finally, with a heartfelt sigh, August joined her again.

And it was more fulfilling than every memory he'd held on to for years.

"I love you," he said.

"I love you back, August," Evie replied with such certainty that he didn't need to hear it again…because it felt completely, utterly right.

WHEN EVIE WOKE UP ALONE the next morning back in her own bed, she couldn't resist stretching her legs out and counting to ten. She felt so good. So perfect.

Okay, she could admit it—she felt like a woman.

For years, she'd felt like a mother, a wife, a single adult in the workforce, worrying about health-care coverage and vacation days.

She'd felt independent and responsible, and, if truth be told, just a little bit lonely.

But none of that was how she felt at the moment. Her breath seemed to come a little bit faster as she realized that she felt completely feminine. Wanted. Loved.

August Meyer was a terrific lover. He'd been her first, and even then they'd shared something special in the midst of all their earnest fumbling. But now, she was bemused to realize that he'd learned a whole lot through the years.

He'd touched her with care. Oh, not like she was made of porcelain and delicate, but as if he wanted to know every part of her intimately.

The muscles in Evie's stomach bunched as she realized he had, indeed, known every bit of her that way. He hadn't been especially gentle or passionately rough. Just…thorough. He'd petted and kissed and caressed her until she'd thought she couldn't take another minute of his attentions, and then…well, he'd gone and done it again.

"Ma ma ma ma ma ma."

"Missy!" she said, seeing her baby toddle in like an ant on a mission. "How's my baby doing?"

"Ma ma ma ma."

"That's right, I'm your momma," she said, reaching down and gently picking up Missy and cuddling her close. Her warm baby was freshly changed and smelled of baby powder and formula.

Oh, now that was something she was going to miss… her mother helping with little things like this. As she put Missy down by her side, her baby giggled, sticking her little feet in the air. That was all the invitation Evie needed to tickle her baby's tummy and watch her squirm.

Missy's bright blue eyes batted and twinkled as they played their tickle game, and Evie was just bending down to kiss her favorite chubby cheeks when Jenna joined them, Neena in tow.

"Momma, you getting up?"

"Soon. I'm just cuddling Missy."

Jenna jumped up onto the bed and then slid in between the sheets next to Evie. "I'll cuddle, too."

Evie reached over and kissed her daughter right smack on her pursed lips. "Good. Sleep well?"

"Uh-huh. Neena did, too."

"You have breakfast yet?"

"Nope. Just some juice. Grandma's been on the phone."

Having a fairly good idea what her mother was talking to the world about, Evie sat up, rested Missy on her lap and then looked at them both. "We need to talk."

Jenna's eyes went serious. "'Kay."

"We're going to leave here in four days to go back home."

Jenna perked right up. "Back to Texas?"

"Yep, it's time, don't you think?"

Jenna looked around the room. "I like it here."

"I know you do," Evie said gently, having no idea what her next words were going to bring. "But, you're a busy girl. You've got soccer and school to get ready for."

New awareness formed in Jenna's eyes. Turning to Missy, she said, "I'm going to be a second-grader."

Missy just kicked her feet, but Evie knew that was a big deal. "You are." Then she took the plunge. "Daddy said he wants to take you school supply shopping."

"Daddy?"

"Da da da da," Missy chirped.

"Yep, I spoke with Daddy last night," Evie explained, taking care to keep her voice open and upbeat. "He misses you."

"I miss him, too." Jenna screwed up her face as she thought a minute more. "Do Grandma and Grandpa know we're gonna leave soon?"

"They do."

"What about August?"

Just hearing his name brought a warm feeling rushing

through her. Just a week or so ago Evie had wondered if Jenna would ever accept him as part of their lives. "August knows, too. He's going to come out soon and visit."

Pure happiness appeared on Jenna's face. "I'm gonna go get my suitcase."

Well, that was that. And her daughter in a nutshell. "Not yet, we won't be leaving until Wednesday."

"But I want to go home and see Daddy and have August visit us."

"Let's go see August today. We'll call Daddy on Monday."

"Okay," she said, trotting out.

When Missy squirmed to be let free, Evie placed her on the floor and quickly slipped on a robe as her toddler carefully walked toward the stairs then started climbing up at the speed of lightning.

So much worry, over in a snap. They were going back to their life. And…it was gonna be okay.

Chapter Twenty

"I'm going to miss you, but you know that, right?"

Evie propped a foot on the top rung of the stool by the granite-covered island and tried not to cry. "I know that."

"I already told your mother that we're coming up there for Halloween. No way am I going to miss trick-or-treating this year. Pictures don't do the girls' costumes justice."

Last year Missy had been a pea pod and Jenna a cat burglar. Both had been as cute as all get out…and Evie had spent most of the night in tears because there was no one at her house to let in trick-or-treaters. "I can't wait for you to be there."

Mike chopped up some broccoli and pulled out a yellow pepper from his produce bag. "Good." After rinsing the pepper under a stream of water, he looked her over. "Have I told you that you look better?"

She couldn't resist throwing his words back in his face. "What? I don't look like hell any longer?"

Her dad didn't even pretend to look shamefaced. "You did look plumb worn-out when you arrived, Evie. I won't deny it."

She wasn't about to deny it, either. "I got on the

scale. I've gained seven pounds since I arrived. My jeans almost fit now."

"Add another seven and you'll be in business."

Evie watched her dad chop up an onion and then finally heat up the wok. This was the kind of thing she missed more than the fun activities or the constant help and emotional support her parents provided.

She missed their time and attention. She missed talking about things that she didn't dare bring up with other people. She missed the casual glances and the way that cooking dinner together became a happy event, not another chore to get through until it was time to relax.

"Sure you and August didn't want to go out, just the two of you tonight? Mom and I are happy to just hang out with the girls."

"No, I wanted us all to be together. You and Mom and Beverly and Tanya and August."

Mike cracked a smile. "Beverly's bringing a cake, but don't let her know I told you."

There was that secret smile on his face again. "What are you up to, Daddy?"

"No good."

"They're here! They're here!" Jenna cried out, scampering into the kitchen like a mini whirling dervish.

"Settle down and don't run."

"Okay, but they're here! And they brought presents!" Jenna said, running right back outside, the screen door slapping shut as she skipped out.

Evie slowly slid off the stool. "Dad? What's going on?"

He waited a second before replying. "We're having a party."

"For who?"

"You, of course." He raised an eyebrow. "Know anyone else who's fixing to turn thirty?"

"My birthday's not for another month."

"But you'll be back in Texas then, so we're celebrating now."

"I told you I didn't want a big deal."

"I kept my word. This party was August's idea," Mike said. "And if you are the woman I know you to be, you're going to smile sweetly and not cause a fuss."

Evie decided to let the manners lesson fall by the wayside since she was still coming to terms with the fact that August was the one who'd decided she needed a birthday party. "Why do you think August would do such a thing?"

"Because I wanted to," the focus of her thoughts said as he walked in and joined them. Then, just as if her father wasn't chopping up vegetables right beside her, August kissed her right on the mouth.

And lingered.

"Wow," Mike said. "Look, you two. I can't leave my wok, so go take that someplace else."

August winked at her. "Gladly."

"Hold up," Evie protested when he pushed her to the family room. "I want to know when you've had time to organize a party."

He kissed her neck, stopping to nuzzle her cheek along the way. "Remember how we decided not to make love again last night?"

He made her breathless just by standing next to her. "I remember."

"And remember how you insisted on going home on Saturday night after—"

She covered his mouth with her palm. No way did she even want a hint of what they'd been doing uttered aloud. "I remember."

"Well, I used all that extra time to make some plans."

"What sort of plans?"

"Let's go see." And with that, August led Evie to the porch. To where Jenna was hopping up and down, and Tanya was holding Missy, and her mom and Beverly were waiting. "Surprise!" they all called out.

That's when she saw the four brightly colored packages and gift bags and the beautiful cake under a clear plastic container. Chocolate, her favorite, with bright pink roses, Jenna's favorite, everywhere on it.

"Oh, my goodness!"

Tears pricked Evie's eyes as she realized how happy she was. And how scared to death she was that things weren't going to work out like she wanted.

Weren't going to be as good as she'd hoped.

"Let's open them up!" Jenna proclaimed, happily leading the way to the table.

In no time, presents were opened and paper and ribbon littered the floor. Next, they ate Mike's dinner and then returned to the living room.

Soon, the very familiar tunes of 1950s rock and roll floated through the room. "This song's called 'Dream Angel,'" Mike told Jenna, who scampered right over to start dancing.

"I'm going to miss this," Evie said when August pulled her into a slow dance as if there was nothing completely crazy about slow dancing to old songs in her parents' living room alongside his sister and mom.

Once more, they fit together, like gloves, or spoons in a drawer, or heck, even the matching salt-and-pepper shakers that the catalog sold.

Evie wasn't picky about the analogy, just that it fit. Just like she and August did.

"We can dance whenever we're together," he whispered into her ear, his breath grazing her neck, sending chill bumps down her spine. And that felt so good.

Until Evie realized that August had inserted a very important word into his very sweet line. Whenever. How was she going to survive knowing she was being pulled in yet another direction?

At her continued silence, August kissed her shoulder. "Don't worry, babe. We'll dance whenever you want to."

It sounded heavenly. Being with him felt heavenly. Bittersweet emotions flowed through her as she realized that for a very long time afterward, nothing would likely be as perfect as that moment.

Even when August came to visit her in Grapevine, things wouldn't be the same. There, she was firmly entrenched in the real world. Work, day care, John, money...all those factors bundled into her life, making her feel crazy and lonely, all at the same time.

"I wanna dance with August!" Jenna called out as she loosened herself from her grandpa's arms and scurried over to August's. And as expected, August held his arms out easily and shooed Evie toward her dad.

"You okay?" her dad whispered as they began a slow waltz around the perimeter of the patio.

"Truth?"

"Of course."

"I don't know."

Sadness and understanding filled her dad's gaze as he looked at her sadly. "I feel the same way," he murmured.

By mutual agreement, they all filed into the kitchen after the spur-of-the-moment dancing and watched Mike as he did the finishing touches in the electric wok. Evie put Missy in her high chair and sat beside her as everyone else got situated.

Tanya took the place next to her. "I feel like I'm about to lose a sister," she said. "After all these years with just occasional visits, we've finally done more than just catch up."

They certainly had. She and Tanya had finally mended old hurts and built bridges between their two worlds. Now the fact that Evie spent her time raising two girls while Tanya dated a string of handsome men didn't matter so much—they'd found more in common than they'd ever dared to feel.

And now it was all getting pulled apart again.

"I'm going to miss you, too, though I feel silly to even think that way. I'll be back here soon, and you can always come to Texas."

Tanya nodded. "I plan to book a ticket soon." Leaning closer, she confided, "I finally told my mom and August that I wanted to sell the dance studio."

"How did that go over?"

Tanya glanced at her mom, who was standing next to the counter, chatting about her dating life with Jan. "Not as badly as I expected. Of course, they both asked why I just now decided to change course in my life."

As Evie thought of all the things that had happened to her over the last two years, she shrugged. "You can't ask why, I've discovered. Sometimes things just happen."

"Like you and August."

"Yep." Evie hoped the peppy optimism in her voice camouflaged the rest of her feelings. She was in full-force panic. What if starting a relationship now was a mistake? What if she started to rely on him?

"Let's promise to stay in touch. There's no reason we can't write each other on e-mail."

"And call."

Tanya clasped her hand. "That's right, and call."

LATER THAT NIGHT, AFTER JENNA and Missy had long been asleep and her parents had gone off to their bed, Evie and August walked out past the patio and down to the beach.

Once again, the moonlight glittered along the horizon, casting shadows in the sand.

He took hold of her hand. "So, your car's all packed."

"Yep. Thanks for helping me this afternoon."

"You sure you need to leave so early in the morning? Maybe we could have breakfast—"

What Evie wanted and what was possible were two different things. "It's a long drive, we both know that. I don't want to drive in the dark."

"I know." Wrapping an arm around her shoulders, he pulled her closer. "I just don't want to let you go."

She closed her eyes and rested her head briefly on his shoulder before bending down and pulling off her Keds. "I hate it, too."

"I'm flying out to see you in four days."

Four days! Surely she could make it through that? "I know, it's hardly any time."

"You'll be in my arms again before we know it."

"So, why do I feel like crying?"

It was only natural to cuddle closer, to want to hide in his arms and wish the rest of the world would go away. They walked farther along, moving back and forth among the dunes, sticking to the shadows, away from the group of teenagers nearby. Beneath their feet, the sand felt gloriously silky and cool.

As he pressed his lips to her brow, he murmured, "We're going to have to work something out." After a brief pause, he said, "I want something permanent, Evie."

Was he asking what she thought he was asking? Marriage? If so, she wasn't ready. He had to know that. She'd finally just gotten hungry again! No way did she want to think about forever. "Let's take things one step at a time."

"All right. I'll respect that, but I don't want to mislead you. My steps are going to be big ones, Ev."

"I'll try to keep up with them," she whispered, right before his lips claimed hers again.

SAYING GOODBYE TO HER parents was just as hard. "I have money, Daddy," Evie protested as he slipped three twenties in her hand.

"Just in case."

"I'm not a child."

"I don't want you to be. I just want you to be safe. Now if something unforeseen happens, you won't have to go on the prowl for a money machine."

"Thank you," she said, knowing that his offer of cash was as tangible as his love. "And thanks for everything."

"I can't believe how quick the month passed," Jan said. "Now, you hang in there. Dad and I were talking about Halloween, but I just don't know if we can wait that long."

"I'll look at my schedule and let you know."

"Good enough." Jan bit her lip. "Promise me that you'll take care of yourself a little better, Evie."

"I'll try."

"You can tell those girls 'no' sometimes, you know."

"I do." Speaking of the girls, Evie turned to them. Each was already buckled up in her car seat, waiting to go.

When she met her oldest daughter's eye, Jenna scowled. "You coming, Momma?"

"There's my cue," Evie laughed.

"Do they need more juice boxes?"

"We don't need a thing. 'Bye." Quickly Evie hugged her parents one last time, stepped aside so they could squeeze the girls, then buckled up, put the van in Reverse and slowly edged out of the driveway.

A lump formed in her throat as she waved one last time to her parents and drove down the street.

And as she made the few right and left turns, she

couldn't help but glance toward August's unit, just in case he was standing there.

But everything was closed and shut up.

Slowly they edged out onto the main road. Past the exit for Cascade Beach. Past the boardwalk and the marina and past the giant Ferris wheel that always broke down.

As she entered the freeway, Evie grinned as she read the billboard announcing that nonstop fun was just two exits away.

"How much longer, Momma?"

"A long while, honey."

"Missy wants her stupid cell phone."

"Then I think you better hand it over and settle in."

"This is gonna take forever," she moaned.

But amazingly, Jenna passed over the toy, Missy squealed in delight and Evie sighed. "Want to listen to Harry Potter?"

"All right, but I feel sad."

"I know. I feel sad, too." And with that, Evie popped in the tape and concentrated on the road home.

Chapter Twenty-One

Her three-bedroom ranch house was exactly how she'd left it—bright, homey, and splashed here and there with a liberal touch of whimsy. Evie had always loved the gleaming white countertops with the blue teapot cabinet pulls in her kitchen.

She'd loved the yellow walls in her family room and the bold red-checked couch in her family room…the girls loved it, too.

So why did it all seem so overly bright and too much all the sudden?

Hefting one of her many tote bags, Evie lugged it past the living room and into her bedroom. Along the way, she peeked into her girls' rooms. Jenna barely looked up from the toys she hadn't seen in a month, and it looked as though Missy hadn't moved from where Evie had laid her down after the drive.

Upon entering her room, Evie breathed deep, then tossed a bag on her bed. For the first time, her private sanctuary brought no relief.

Her bedroom had been the first room of the house she'd decorated. At the time she'd been so thankful for her job at the catalog, she'd bought many of their discontinued items for next to nothing and had created a Parisian feel, with a lace comforter, pale, shell-pink walls and bistro knickknacks. It all went well with her queen-size sleigh bed and cherry armoire. In a way, it had been a symbol of independence. A part of her rebellion against marriage and John. John, who liked neutrals and stripes. Nothing too fussy.

But now it felt too feminine, too *single*. "This is the bedroom of a single woman," she told the antique doll she'd placed in a glass box on her dresser. "This is the bedroom of a woman who is not looking for love."

More likely, it was the room of a woman buried in the past.

But after one month, that wasn't her anymore. She was completely head over heels in love again…or maybe for the first time? To a man who couldn't relocate. The sense of irony would have been laughable if she wasn't so tired.

She would have loved nothing better than to curl up on the bed with Missy and try and forget about all her problems, but unfortunately, this wasn't Florida, and there was no longer anyone around to help her.

Forcing herself to stay on task, Evie lugged another bag inside, this time to her tiny laundry closet off the kitchen. But when she unzipped the bag and pulled out a beach towel, the fresh, tart scent of sand and the sea brought back memories of another place.

Of where her heart was now.

When were things going to be easier? Resolutely, she tossed the towels and a bunch of shorts and T-shirts in the washing machine, poured in a liberal amount of Tide and pressed Start.

Next she ransacked the cupboards for something to eat for the kids. Though Jenna hadn't started complaining about being hungry, Evie knew that when the hunger pains did hit Jenna, they'd be loud and demanding. "Spa-ghettiOs, okay?" she called out.

"Uh-huh."

"Coming right up." As she opened the can and dumped the contents into a microwave-safe bowl, Evie wished she was hungry, but there were no longer any fresh muffins or baby quiches or bowls of fruit on the table. Only cans of soup and mac and cheese until she could get to the grocery store.

That meant a trip to the store with both of them, which meant an hour-long errand could run to two hours if she wasn't careful.

As the washing machine clicked on behind her and the SpaghettiOs warmed up, she sat down and tried to write a list.

But all she could think about was grilled fish from Monterey's on the pier or corn dogs on a stick.

It was a relief when the phone rang and a true blessing when she heard the sweetest, sexiest voice on the planet.

"You okay?"

She was now. "August. Hi."

"How long have you been home?"

"Almost an hour. Long enough to wish I was some-where else," she admitted.

"It feels like you've been gone forever. I went to see your parents, and found your dad eating mac and cheese on the back porch, looking like someone stole his puppy."

She laughed at the vision. "I know the feeling."

"I kind of felt that way, too."

"Me, too. This place has never seemed so empty."

"What are you doing now?"

"Heating up SpagehettiOs and doing laundry. You?"

"I just went for a swim."

"In the ocean?"

"Yeah."

If Evie closed her eyes, she knew she could conjure August up, wet from the sea, his arms and shoulders hard and muscular, his green eyes a little red because saltwater always stung them. "Feel good?"

"I guess. I can't wait to see you, Evie."

"Me, too." Just to make him smile, she intentionally added some levity. "When you come out, I'm going to take you out for ice cream."

"Can't wait."

She swallowed hard.

August, too, seemed like he was searching for things to say. "So. Did the girls do okay in the van?"

"They did as well as can be expected. That stupid cell phone is Missy's favorite toy."

His laugh floated through the line, warming her insides. "You sound like Jenna."

She chuckled, too. "Believe me, I was as irritated as she was."

They talked for a little bit more, August telling her about a family reunion group that had half of his staff running every minute to see to their needs. "Hey, I'll see you in two days," he murmured when his cell phone rang.

"See you," she whispered, just as her line beeped, signaling another call. "'Bye," she said, then clicked to the other man in her life.

John.

"Evie, you home okay?"

"Yep."

"How are the girls?"

"They're good." Forcing herself to talk, even though all she wanted to do was sit on the couch and cry, Evie added, "Jenna's in her room and I'm making her some SpaghettiOs."

"She loves those." He paused. "So, is it still okay if I come by to get them tomorrow?"

"Of course. I'd invite you by tonight, but I'm afraid you'd just get two crabby children."

He laughed. "I'll pass on that. Besides, I've already got plans," he said after a pause.

Evie now had a pretty good idea that "plans" was actually Terri. "Well, my plans involve putting my feet up and watching TV."

"See you tomorrow at ten?"

"They'll be ready. 'Bye, John."

"'Bye. Hey, Evie?"

"Yeah?"

"Thanks for coming back early."

"You're welcome," she said, then hung up. Not wanting to sit and stew over the feelings that were flooding over her at the moment, she called out, "Jenna, come eat."

Jenna trotted out with Neena. "I'm hungry."

"Good, because there's a bowl of SpaghettiOs here."

And as she sat down at the kitchen table, Evie wondered if she'd ever felt more alone.

IF A TINY PART OF EVIE secretly wished that the girls would look at John and rebel and kick and scream and say they didn't want to see him, she was sorely disappointed.

In fact, the girls couldn't have been more excited. Jenna was standing at the window, her little backpack filled with pictures and drawings and a T-shirt that said All my daughter brought me back from Florida was a stupid T-shirt.

When John drove up, Jenna pulled open the door and tore out to hug her daddy.

John scooped her up and held on just as close. With a trace of envy, Evie watched them chat, then approach her front door, John already with his eyes glued to Missy, who had toddled to the doorway and was peeking out.

"Hey, Evie," he said, before putting down one girl and picking up another.

"Da!" Missy called out.

"Missy!"

Evie was close enough to see the sheer bliss on John's face when he cuddled Missy closer.

And then the girls were ready to go. "Hold on, now," John told Jenna with enough force to give Evie a good idea that he, too, had been at her demanding mercy more than just a time or two.

Finally there was a moment when she and John were looking at each other directly. Like they used to. His blue eyes skimmed over her. "Evie, you look different."

"It's called sleep and corn dogs."

"It looks good on you."

She couldn't help but laugh. "You sound surprised."

"Not surprised, just glad."

"Thanks. Um, how are you?"

He shrugged. "Good. I finally got that business plan out, so things are going a little more smoothly. So, you're going to have company?"

"Yeah. August."

"I guess you two have gotten close."

"Very."

Surprise filled his gaze again, but it didn't come across as anything other than curiosity. "I'm glad."

"Daddy?"

"I'm coming, Jen," he called out to their daughter, who was standing impatiently in the front yard. Looking at Evie, he said, "Terri's going to join us for pizza tonight."

Obviously, they'd both found happiness. "I hope you have a good time."

He stepped away, but then backtracked. "Is this weird?"

She looked at her feet. "I don't know. I never imagined we'd be divorced, but since we are, I think we're doing pretty good. I'm glad we get along."

"Me, too." Relief, and the same stark awareness, flew into his expression. "I'll call you on Sunday afternoon to see when I can drop the girls off."

"Okay."

"Daddy?"

"I hear you, Jenna. And watch your tone."

Almost amused, Evie watched Jenna's bottom lip stick out.

When they were gone, Evie went back in, looked at the pile of laundry and the stack of dishes. But instead of feeling overwhelmed, she was invigorated.

August was due in twenty-four hours. In a day's time, she'd be in his arms again, and more than ever, she could hardly wait.

"YOU ALL PACKED?"

"Just about, Mom," August said for what had to be the twentieth time.

"Do you think this is a good idea, visiting Evie in Texas?"

"You're saying Texas like it's Australia, Mom. It's just a two-hour plane ride."

"You know what I mean. If you go see her, things won't get back to normal."

"I don't think I want things how they used to be, Mom."

Beverly Meyer sat down next to him on the wooden bench on his back porch. "What are you hoping for? To win her back?"

"We're a couple. There is no winning her back." Taking a closer look at his mom, it occurred to August that there was more going on than he'd previously realized. "What's going on here?"

"Harmonious Haven isn't all it's cracked up to be," she finally stated, shoulders slumped.

"What happened?"

"Most of the men are losers."

"Why do you say that?"

"One man asked how much money your father left me."

August bit back his anger, as well as a healthy dose of "I told you so's." "I hope you didn't tell him."

"I didn't tell him a thing." With a sigh, she added, "It's just so hard, figuring out who to trust. Your father was such a good man."

"Dad was the best," August agreed. "Are you taking care of yourself?"

"Of course. I went to Tanya's stretch-and-tone class this morning."

"Are you upset about the dance studio?"

"Not as much as I thought I would be. Life moves on, you know?" Before he could answer, she grasped his hand. "August, I like Evie. I like her parents. I think Jenna and Missy are adorable. She's done a good job with those girls."

"I agree."

"Tanya's finally starting to get settled. I thought we were all getting along okay."

"I think we are, Mom."

"I just hope you don't do something foolish."

"Like what? Fall in love?"

Hope and confusion filled her eyes. "Have you fallen in love?"

"I know I have. I wouldn't be chasing Evie around the country if I didn't."

"I hope she doesn't break your heart."

"She won't."

AFTER SHE LEFT, AUGUST THREW some clothes in a duffel and wished he could pick up a flight within an hour. The time apart wasn't making his heart fonder. Instead it was causing old memories to resurface. Though ten years had passed, August couldn't help but remember just how hurt he'd been when she'd told him that since she wasn't pregnant, they didn't have to worry about each other.

How it was time for them both to move on. And she had.

Chapter Twenty-Two

She was not eighteen years old. She was a grown woman with an ex-husband and two children. Grown women didn't feel all breathless and excited when their boyfriends were coming to visit them.

Right?

Wrong. Evie was an extreme bundle of nerves...and once more, she kind of liked the feeling. As yet another line of people paraded up the escalator from the airport gates, Evie scanned the faces, knowing that it was probably too early to see him. But, just in case...

She'd been like that all day. And yesterday. She'd thought she'd feel strange when John picked up the girls and warned her that he was going to take them to the movies with Terri. But instead she'd felt glad that he had someone. Glad John had met someone who made him feel the way she did with August. Because at the moment, she was incredibly sorry for anyone who had never felt as young and carefree...and silly as she did right at that moment.

Once again she scanned the escalator, looking for the unmistakable honey-colored hair, deep tan and green-as-grass eyes. Looking for those broad shoulders. And then, well, there he was.

Of course, he didn't say a word. Didn't even lift a hand. He didn't need to. All he needed to do was direct his gaze her way and smile and she was toast.

And because no one she knew was standing nearby to see her act way too childish, Evie ran straight to his arms when he stepped off the escalator.

As usual, he felt wonderful. Without waiting a beat, he claimed her lips, pressing his warm, wide palm against her shoulder blades as he deepened their kiss, just like something out of the movies. And though a couple of people around them giggled and whispered, Evie found she didn't care. All that really mattered was that he was real, in her arms, and out of her daydreams.

Evie clung to his forearms. "I missed you."

"I missed you, too. I can't believe it's only been three days since I saw you, it feels like it's been two weeks."

"I'm so glad you said that." That was why she'd fallen in love with August. He said the kind of things that made her believe that she, too, could open herself up to him. "What do you want to do first?"

He held up the duffel bag he'd obviously carried on the flight. "Get out of here."

"All right, then." Stepping out into the bright Texas sun, she slipped her sunglasses back over her eyes and noticed August doing the same. "Are you hungry?"

He glanced over at her. "Are you?"

Once again she felt like everything had two meanings. The question was, was she ready to dive into those double entendres or to play it safe? Safety won. "I could go for Mexican food. You ready to try some Tex-Mex?"

"Always."

She turned her vehicle toward the parking lot entrance. Then was glad she was at a full stop when he finished that thought. "I'm not ready for Tex-Mex just yet." Claiming her hand, he said, "Let's go back to your place, Evie. All I want to do is kiss you again."

She wanted that, too. Actually, she wanted a whole lot more than that. "I only live fifteen minutes away."

Leaning back on the leather seat, he skimmed a finger down her neck, over her bare shoulder, along her arm. "Good."

Her body shivered in response. Evie knew if ever she was in danger of getting a traffic ticket, now would be the time.

Thank goodness she exited the freeway and negotiated the way to her subdivision without any trouble, because at the moment, August's fingers were brushing her bare thigh and every nerve ending was zipping upward, tightening her stomach, making her imagine all sorts of things they'd be doing in mere minutes. Oh, why hadn't she just worn a pair of jeans?

Because she'd wanted this, her body said in response. She'd wanted it in a way she hadn't ever wanted much else.

As if reading her mind, August played a little more with the ruffle at the edge of her skirt, which he'd managed to hike up to midthigh. He was fiddling with the hem, brushing a calloused finger along her supersensitive skin, skimming the elastic of her cotton underwear. His fingers were just light enough to make her want to jump out of her seat, just enough to wish she was brave enough to start caressing his thighs. Of course, then she'd surely get in an accident.

After stopping at the light, she turned right. Now they were only minutes from her subdivision. Five minutes, tops.

August removed his hand, leaving her whole bare leg exposed and every part of her throbbing.

Evie bit her lip and hoped he wouldn't notice.

"I haven't seen this dress before. You didn't bring it to Florida, did you?"

Was he really focusing on the *dress?* "No. It has to be ironed...." Her voice drifted off, unable to think of any more words. Luckily, she pulled into her driveway, pushed the garage door opener and edged inside. There. She did it.

No wreck, no dangerous swerving. She really did deserve a prize for that. "Well, we're here."

He looked around. "Nice garage," he said.

She laughed. "One day I'm going to organize this place. But you know how that kind of thing was never my strong point."

"Mm-hmm." He dropped a kiss on her bare shoulder just as she'd pressed the electric doorlock button and pulled out the keys.

But August didn't seem to be in any hurry to exit her vehicle. Slowly, he pressed his whole palm on her bare thigh. The thigh that was practically quivering from all his attentions. Warm heat slid through her skin. Snaked its way up her legs, meeting in a place that hadn't seen a whole lot of action in a very long time. Her thighs tightened, her body got all quivery and warm, luxurious feelings tightened her nipples, making her mouth go dry.

So much for acting all relaxed and easygoing.

He noticed. With a look of interest, August slid her skirt up a little higher. "Am I making you nervous, Evie?"

"Not nervous."

He kissed her neck. Darted his tongue along her earlobe. And pushed her poor skirt even farther upward. Now both her legs were bare, right there in the driver's seat of her Mazda minivan.

Lord have mercy.

August chuckled. "So, what am I making you feel?"

"I...I don't know."

"Sure you do. Tell me, Evie."

Evie stared at him, bemused. Since when did August Meyer talk dirty in minivans? Since when did that kind of talk set her body on edge, making her wish for things she'd never done with John?

Yes, he was making her nervous—not that he needed to know that.

Edging to her left, she opened up her door and scrambled from his grasp. "It's so warm out here, we're going to burn up if we stay in the garage much longer." With a quick glance out toward the street, she hoped Mrs. Reynolds wasn't watching from her window, because her skirt was twisted and fighting its way back down her thighs.

August pushed the garage door button. "I guess you're right," he said, finally opening his door, too.

With easy motions, August got out of his side, picked up his duffel, stepped closer and pulled her into his arms. She held on tight and kissed him back.

There was something about kissing a man in the shaded confines of a garage. It felt sneaky and unfamiliar, once again heightening all of her senses as his cologne mixed in with the scent of grass and gasoline. She stood on her tiptoes and explored him further until it was August who pulled away. "Let's go inside."

She followed him in, switched on the entryway light and, before she could say anything, he took her in his arms and kissed her like there was no tomorrow. Evie was practically plastered against him, her smooth legs gliding along his thicker, hairy ones. Her chest was pressed against his solid chest. And his hands were massaging her back, dissolving knots, making her languid and supple and perfect.

How did August do that, anyway?

"Where's your bed, Evie?" His voice was thick with passion, husky from their kisses.

"Down the hall." Without another word, she took his hand and led him to her room, opened the door, and was glad she hadn't remembered to turn off her ceiling fan. A light breeze beckoned them in.

August looked around, but didn't comment.

For her part, Evie didn't offer a single apology for how feminine and lacy it was. Didn't think to wonder if he liked it or not. Didn't speculate if she should turn on a light or flip off the fan.

Because all August seemed to want to do was slide her dress in a whole other direction. This time, he started from the top and worked his way down. Edging the narrow straps off her shoulders, over her breasts, down her torso, along her legs, until it pooled on the floor around her red toenails.

"Evie," he murmured, his gaze tender and appreciative.

She helped him pull off his shirt.

And when he pulled her down on the bed with him, reached for her, and they finally did everything they'd wanted to for the last four days.

And, just as in Florida, making love with August was worth waiting for. Special. Perfect.

Chapter Twenty-Three

"Take me around Grapevine," August said two hours later, after they'd cuddled and showered and hopped back on that rose satin bedspread one more time.

"I thought you just wanted me to feed you Tex-Mex," Evie teased as they got back in the car.

He grinned right back. "I want that, too." His look was vintage August—sexy and hot, full of surprises and gently loving.

"Isn't that just like a man? You want it all."

He raised a hand. "I'm offering no excuses."

"You don't need any," she said, and began the tour.

So she gave him everything Grapevine and the surrounding suburbs of Dallas had to offer. They drove north on I-635, past the giant Bass Pro Shop and the bright and shiny Grapevine Mills shopping area. She took him downtown to the JFK Memorial, where the schoolbook depository was, to the beautiful statues of the racing stallions in Las Colinas. She drove him by Crowd Pleasers Catalog, just off the beltway in Carrollton. And, at his request, Evie brought August inside to meet everyone.

It was no surprise that everyone fell in love with him. He was charming and handsome, and Evie caught Sue, the

Crowd Pleasers owner, fixating on the way August kept Evie's hand firmly grasped in his own.

Just when they were about to return to the car and August was chatting with the receptionist, Sue pulled her to one side. "Wow, Evie. You told me he was handsome, but not that he was built like a Greek god," she quipped, fanning her cheeks dramatically. "If I wasn't already taken, I'd flirt outrageously."

"I'm glad you're married, then." Evie smiled.

Sue looked him over once more. "Is he treating you well?"

"Very well. He's a good guy."

"I bet. He's a keeper, Evie." After another knowing look, she said, "You *are* going to keep him, right?"

Because she couldn't tell the future, and had no desire to even try anymore, Evie said, "If I do, I'll let you know."

When August joined them, Sue ignored all sense of decorum and began to interrogate August. "So, what kind of business are you in?"

August stole a quick, curious look at Evie before answering. "My family owns a resort. I run it."

"Are you an only child?"

"No, I have a sister."

"Does she work at the resort, too?"

"Sometimes. Is there anything else you need to know?"

The question held a hint of sarcasm in it, but that didn't seem to stop Sue. Instead of looking shamed, she pulled her shoulders back. "Actually, I did want—"

"Hold now," Evie interjected before Sue could say another word. "I think it's time for us to get going."

"If you're sure."

"I'm sure…unless you want to see his teeth, too, Sue?"

Undeterred, Sue shook her head. "Nope. From what I can tell, his teeth look perfectly fine."

Evie groaned. "Let's go," she said, shooing August out before Sue forgot herself even further and started flirting with him.

After they were buckled up, August raised an eyebrow. "What was that all about?"

"Nothing. It's just, well, Sue is hoping you'll move here." When his eyes widened, she backtracked. "Don't worry, I'm not trying to pressure you."

"Only Sue."

Evie didn't know what to say. Sue had been a little too nosy, but over the last two years, her boss had also been the ultimate lifesaver. Sue's job offer and subsequent friendship had been really appreciated. In addition, her exuberant personality had lifted Evie's spirits more than a time or two. "She just wants me happy."

"I want you happy, too, Evie."

"I'm happy with you," she said. After a moment's hesitation, she took him to Grapevine Lake, the boating area for northern Dallas/Fort Worth. "I know this is nothing compared to the ocean, but it's kind of a nice place when you consider Dallas is a landlocked city."

August actually looked interested. "What's over here?" he asked, pointing to a large shopping complex.

Briefly Evie told him about the new developments that had recently sprung up. "People are hoping this will be kind of an interesting venue for future conferences," she explained.

"I think it's a great spot. There's a rusticness about this place that's charming and unexpected."

His words took her by surprise, but Evie figured she shouldn't have been. After all, vacation resorts and conference centers were his family's business. "Are you ready to eat now?"

"Yep, I'm starving."

She took him to Tia's, a local favorite, and sat across from him, sipping an iced tea while he discovered the wonders of Tex-Mex burritos, rice and beans.

Finally, they drove back to her place. "I kind of feel funny, having you here and not worrying about the girls," she admitted. "For the first time, I'm not working, not being a mom, not cleaning house…and not sitting by myself, wondering when the girls will get back home."

"There's more to you than those things, Evie. You need to remember that."

"I don't forget when you're around," she admitted softly. "You make me remember that I'm more." She squeezed his hands, enjoying the feel of how she was held so securely in between both of his palms.

Surprisingly, August didn't reply, which made the sweet moment a little off-kilter. His silence reminded Evie that there were so many words left unsaid between them.

When they were back on her street, August spoke again. "It's pretty around here. To be honest, I wasn't sure what to expect from the Grapevine area."

"I like it here a lot," she admitted. "I love how green it all is. I love living close to a big city."

"I guess Texas has a lot more going for it than I thought."

Evie chuckled. Glancing at the clock, she saw it was after seven. A soft glow filtered through her levered blinds, muting the color, making the brick-red paint look warmer and cozy.

Their day had been perfect. Easy and relaxed. When he leaned back against the cushions of her couch, she couldn't help but notice just how his T-shirt pulled against his broad shoulders. "So, would you like to watch TV?"

"Sure." He held out an arm for her, and Evie snuggled against him.

After flipping around the channels, they found a couple of sitcoms and half watched them. At least Evie only half watched them. The other part of the time, she let her mind drift back to blue waters and salty air. Back to warm sand between her toes and the rush of the tide coming in.

Evidently, August brought feelings of relaxation and happiness wherever he was. Evie didn't know if she'd ever felt so at peace.

"I'm getting sleepy," August said. "I was up late last night, trying to get things done so I wouldn't be on the phone the whole time I was here."

"I appreciate that," she said, realizing for the first time how different he'd been around her than John had. With John, his BlackBerry and cell phone had always accompanied them. Throughout the day, she hadn't noticed August on it once. "You didn't need to check in?"

"Tanya would kill me if I did. Besides, I don't want anything to take me from you, Evie. I've waited too long for this."

Warning bells rang loud in her ear. Evie felt as if she should say something, but she wasn't sure what to add. What were they going to do? "I, um—"

"Let's go to bed, Evie."

"All right," she said. Walking by his side, Evie could almost forget that they still hadn't ever talked of the future. Still hadn't thought about what they would do when Monday came and they were apart again.

AUGUST LIKED GRAPEVINE. MAYBE because it was unfamiliar and he was intrigued by the idea of opening a place where everything he did wouldn't be judged against the way his father had always done it.

He liked Evie's home. It suited her—the bright colors, the clean lines, the whole feeling of love and warmth that surrounded him from the moment he'd entered the front door.

But most of all, he really enjoyed Evie's company. Though she seemed slightly more tense than at the end of their time together in Florida, she also seemed completely in her element. That Texas accent was thicker than ever. Her bearing was a little more proper, her stance and walk more of a polished city gal than a beach bum.

August enjoyed the feeling of letting her be in control. It wasn't a hardship; he had no need to be in charge of their time together. Besides, from what he gathered, he was sure she'd done too little of that in recent years.

When he woke up, Evie was still sound asleep next to him, her arms flung up over her head as if she was in mid-stretch. After throwing on a pair of jeans, he padded into the kitchen to make a pot of coffee, then set to work making her breakfast.

He'd just put a pad of butter on her stack of pancakes when she appeared. "August?" she said sleepily, her hair a tangled mess down her back and her cheeks flushed from sleep.

"Go back to bed, sugar. I was about to bring these to you."

"Breakfast in bed? I haven't gotten that treat in a long while."

"You won't get it today if you don't listen. Go on back, now."

Her gray eyes widened and warmed with something close to surprise, or maybe it was simply shyness, but she nodded and padded back down the hall.

When he arrived in her room, she'd taken off her robe and was waiting with just a white sheet covering her chest. "You look pretty," he said when their eyes met again.

"Thanks," she replied.

As she cut part of the stack with her fork and took a bite, he sat on the side of her bed. "Do you have plans for us today?"

"Not too much. I have to get the girls from John around two o'clock."

"So I'll get to meet him?"

"If you want," she said slowly. "If you don't, you could stay here. It shouldn't take me too—"

"I want."

"Oh. Okay."

"Sometime soon we need to talk about us."

"I don't know what to say, August. Things between us haven't changed all that much. I still have my life here, you have yours in Florida. Those things can't change."

"One of us could move."

"You would move?"

"I've thought about it," he said slowly.

"I didn't think I could ask you to relocate."

"If I was honest, I'm not sure that I'm exactly ready to do that, yet. My life's been there. But I've been thinking about it."

Evie took another bite. "Well, I don't think you can just up and move, either. I could tell John that it's my prerogative to move the girls, but I don't know if it's in the girls' best interests. You could tell your family that you're going to be neglecting the family business and your mother's health, all for our relationship. But I don't think that's the type of people we are."

They weren't. Maybe that was why neither of them had ever pushed harder back in college. Both of them liked to do what was expected of them, especially when it came to pleasing their families.

That wasn't to say August had a problem standing up to people at work or in other parts of his life. He'd stood up plenty of times when it had been necessary…but this wasn't necessary, was it?

"I can't stand the thought of losing you again."

"You won't." Placing her plate on the table to her left, she grasped his hand. "August, I've had two relationships in my life. You and John. I'm not going to fall apart if I have to eat dinner alone or don't get breakfast in bed on a regular basis."

His lips curved. "And only have sex every couple of weeks?"

She laughed. "I've made love more times this weekend than I care to admit I did during the last few months with John."

"I was teasing," he murmured, brushing a strand of hair away from her very pretty neck. "Maybe we can make things work out. You could come visit me every other month. I'll do the same thing."

"I'll talk to John…maybe he can take the girls for long weekends and I'll run to see you. We can make it work, if we really want it to."

"I really want it to."

"Me, too."

His gaze darted to her lips. "That's what I wanted to hear," he murmured before he bent down to kiss her, softly at first, then with more passion.

Without words, he coaxed a response from her, deepening their connection, trying to tell her in as many ways as possible how much she meant to him. How happy he was to have her in his life again.

He'd just pulled the sheet down and was making his way down her body when the phone rang.

Evie frowned at the phone as it rang again.

"Ignore it," he said.

"I can't." Obviously frustrated, Evie glanced at the

caller ID, then froze. "That's John's cell phone." With two motions, she had the sheet back up and the phone to her ear. "John?"

Fighting back an unfamiliar surge of jealousy, August scooted away, giving her space, trying to erase the tension he felt. The last thing Evie needed was to have him acting like an adolescent.

"What? Oh, my gosh. Where? Okay. No, no I'm fine. I'll be right there." With a look of despair, she set the receiver back into the cradle.

"What happened?"

"It's Jenna. Oh August, there's been an accident."

Chapter Twenty-Four

Evie was sure the emergency room doors were on the blink. "They're not opening," she said, pushing the handle with all her might. "Why aren't they working?"

"They are, Ev," August said, his voice slow and steady. "Pull." With an easy motion, he pulled on the door, then stepped to one side, staying in place as an elderly lady carefully moved herself and her walker through the portal.

Evie didn't wait for anything, though she knew she was being rude. She pushed her way through, knowing she was overreacting but not knowing how to not be a basket case. Frantically, she scanned the doorway, and felt like crying when she didn't automatically see John. *Where was John?*

But instead of her ex-husband, it was August who stood by her side, his presence sure and steady. "Slow down, Ev."

"I can't slow down. Jenna's in here somewhere and I don't have a single clue where. Don't you understand?"

August visibly bit back a retort.

Shamefaced, Evie saw that he was plainly doing his best to remember that Evie was concerned about her daughter, not his feelings. "I'm sorry. I'm having a hard time dealing with all of this."

"It's okay."

But Evie knew he was disappointed that she was taking out her frustrations on him. As best she could, she tried to roll the feeling of guilt from her shoulders. If she wasn't careful, a blinding headache would surface and then she'd be no good to anyone. "I'll be better as soon as—" She interrupted herself when she finally saw John.

As always, he looked like a model. Tall and lithe, handsome enough for a *GQ* cover. Though no smile was in evidence today. Instead, his expression was grim, his blue eyes troubled. In his arms was Missy and a washcloth. The washcloth looked wet and well-chewed. Beside him stood a pretty, well-coiffed lady with black, wavy hair. Terri. After briefly nodding in her direction, Evie raced to his side. "John, I came as fast as I could."

"Thanks," John said, relief in his expression and a tired smile on his face.

August took a deep breath as he approached the trio. Though he wasn't jealous—obviously both Evie and John had moved on—there was a new awareness that there would always be another man of importance in Evie's life. August was man enough to admit that that was going to take some getting used to.

When Missy saw him, she beamed around the wet washcloth. "Gus! Gus!" she blurted.

"Hey, sweetie."

Evie turned to August. "John, this is August. August Meyer."

John held out a hand. "Hey, how you doing? This is Terri."

She nodded politely as they did the round of introductions again.

"I'm sorry about Jenna," August said.

"Thanks. It was one of those crazy things, you know?" John ran his fingers through his hair. "I'm sorry, Evie. Jenna was riding just fine so I decided to go fool with the hose in the front yard. Next thing I knew, she turned a corner too fast and wiped out."

"Poor thing."

"Yep. As soon as she fell, she started crying for all she was worth. And then, as soon as I saw the position her leg was in, I knew she was in big trouble. I scooped her up in one arm, Missy in the other, and plopped them both in the car, both of them crying loud enough for the whole city of Dallas to give me dirty looks." The corners of his eyes crinkled. "I won't be sorry if I never have to go through that again."

Evie shook her head. "Sometimes when they both start crying, I'm sure they're in some kind of secret contest, to see who can wail the loudest."

"It would have been a dead-on tie today."

"Where is Jenna?"

"Getting dressed. Our daughter has suddenly decided she's too old for her father to see her in her underwear. I got sent out here to wait."

Terri smiled at Evie. "She didn't want my help, either, though I offered."

Evie chuckled. "I'm not surprised."

"Mr. Randall?" a nurse called out. "Your daughter's ready for you now."

After exchanging a knowing glance with Terri, August held his arms out for Missy. "How about if we stay here with Missy while you two go see Jenna?"

Evie already had her hand on the door. "You sure you don't mind?"

"Nope."

"Thanks," John said as he handed over Missy, then

guided Evie through the throng of people standing and sitting in the large room. August felt his cheek tic as he noticed how John took the opportunity to touch the small of Evie's back as they turned the corner.

"Gus gus gus," Missy blurped.

"That's right. I'm Gus. You're Missy. And that's Terri."

"Tree."

Terri smiled. "I'm almost going to miss being called that when she grows up," she said with a laugh.

Now that Evie was gone, August took a moment to study Terri a little more closely. At first glance, she looked to be the polar opposite of Evie. Her hair was shiny and almost black, setting off a stunning pair of hazel eyes. Artfully applied makeup showed off her full lips. A crisp, white button-down and neat jeans accentuated a generous figure.

When she started talking, August couldn't help but be charmed; Terri had the accent of every man's dreams, a slow Texas drawl that set a man's thoughts to lazy days and long evenings by a river.

She was amazingly easy to talk to. They spoke about the fantastic growth in the Dallas/Fort Worth area and the many opportunities she'd had in corporate real estate.

He was just telling her about Silver Shells when John, Evie and Jenna appeared, Jenna in a wheelchair and her left leg in a bright pink cast.

Missy's eyes lit up. "Na! Na!"

"Hi, August!" Jenna said.

August gently hugged her. "I like your cast."

"Thanks."

While Evie stood to one side, August noticed that John had moved directly to Terri's side. Clearly John had definitely moved on. "She was a brave girl," John commented.

Jenna tucked her chin to her chest. "I was almost brave. I cried when I fell."

"I would have cried, too," Terri said. "But now you've got a special story to tell, don't you? You're a famous daredevil bike rider!" When Jenna laughed, Terri squeezed her shoulder. "You okay, darlin'?"

"Yep."

Finally, after Evie signed some paperwork, they all made their way to the parking lot, John pushing Jenna's wheelchair. August stood to one side while Evie and John discussed schedules. Finally it was decided that Evie would take the girls on home and John would stop by later with Jenna's toys and overnight bag.

AS SOON AS THEY GOT HOME, Evie helped Jenna to the living room, and got her settled on her bed. To her relief, August did a fine job of helping with Missy, even going so far as to fix up a bottle for her in the kitchen.

A few minutes later, he brought her a mug of hot tea. "Take a sip," he whispered. "Missy's half-asleep on the rug and Jenna's almost there."

With some surprise, Evie realized she'd been staring at her girls with all her might, yet hardly seeing either of them at all. She felt stunned and mentally and physically exhausted.

And a large part of her felt completely to blame. She should have been at the hospital more quickly. She shouldn't have been lying in August's arms when Jenna was in trouble.

August sat down next to her. "You better?"

"No. August, I feel like the worst mother in the world."

"How do you figure that? You weren't even there when Jenna fell off her bike."

"That's why...I *should* have been there."

To her dismay, August chuckled. "Accidents happen, Evie. Even John said that."

Hearing her feelings ridiculed made her lash out. "You don't understand, August. You're not a parent."

"I don't need to be one to understand that parents can't shelter their kids twenty-four/seven. Evie, I broke my arm when I was eight. No one expected my mother to have been in the tree with me."

"I feel like I should have been more worried about her. From the moment I saw you on the escalator, I hardly gave my girls a second thought."

"John was with them, and John's a good guy. Anyway, you could have been at work when she was with a baby-sitter. Why does what you were doing or who you were with matter?"

It just did. With some surprise, Evie realized that a decision had been made. She couldn't have it all, and she shouldn't even try. Something had to be given up, and there was only one option. "Maybe we need to take more time with our relationship. Take things more slowly."

"Slowly? We've known each other for years. We've spent the last month reacquainting ourselves. That's pretty slow, Ev."

It didn't matter that her head knew he was right. Her heart was mixed up. "I just don't know what I would have done if this had happened when I was in Florida. I don't know how I can ever leave the girls and go a whole half a country away."

"Evie, let's talk about this, you're just reacting to your feelings…."

"There's nothing to talk about. I would never be able to be so far away from the girls while they're with John."

"I sure as hell think there's something to talk about. First, calling the distance from Florida to Texas a half a country is stretching it a bit. Secondly, they'd be with their father, not some random babysitter. Don't you think you should put some trust in him?"

She ignored his reasoning. "Now I know why John wanted me back early. *Now I get it.*" Deliberately softening her voice, Evie said, "When she hurts, I hurt," trying to get him to understand. "The only thing that makes it better is knowing that I'm nearby."

Just the thought of how she would have felt, hearing about Jenna's accident from a thousand miles away, made her palms sweat. "I'm sorry, but I was wrong."

"Evie, you don't know what you're saying. Why don't you think about this some?"

Though her head was telling her that August hadn't meant the words like they came out, everything inside of her rebelled. Never again was she going to let any man tell her she didn't know her own mind. "I do know what I'm saying."

Something left August's eyes. He stepped back and ran a hand through his hair. "I guess you do." He pulled out his cell phone. "Let me make some calls and see when the next flight is."

"You don't need to leave this instant."

"Oh, yeah, I do." He looked away for a moment before speaking. "I've spent half my life waiting for you. I was ready to do whatever it took to have a relationship with you, Evie. I wanted to marry you."

"August, I wanted those things, too."

"Did you, Evie?" And with that, he turned away and started punching numbers in his cell phone.

And Evie, instead of feeling like Mother of the Year for putting her children first, was feeling like Poor Relationship Material once again.

And once again, the feeling sucked.

Chapter Twenty-Five

August hadn't appreciated being fifteen enough. Back when he was in high school, his stress had revolved around getting into college, playing football and swimming the two-hundred-meter freestyle in under two minutes.

Oh, he'd written Evie and dated a few girls off and on. One time he'd gotten really sick and had been admitted into the hospital for a couple of days. That had been rough. But over all, he'd only worried about himself and his needs.

Now he had to worry about everyone else's. At the moment, he was worrying about his mother's problems. And at the moment, he'd rather be worrying about anything else. Well, anything besides the fact that Evie was gone from his life and that his heart felt as if it had been smashed into a dozen pieces.

"Mom, it will be okay," he murmured. Again.

"Oh, I know it will be. One day," she replied, giving into tears. "I just never thought I'd be so sad."

He hadn't thought she would be, either. Reaching behind him, he yanked a box of Kleenex from the table next to the couch and set it in front of her. "Here."

"Thanks," she murmured, right before she blew hard into the tissue.

"Mom, Wayne Peterson is a jerk. I'm pretty sure all orthodontists are. I mean, who enjoys dealing with other people's teeth?"

"W—Wayne did."

As she wiped her eyes again, August sighed. "Oh, Mom."

"Wayne said I was too uptight." After blowing her nose in a wad of Kleenex, she added, "He likes riding Harleys!"

"I'm glad you didn't get on his bike."

"Oh, I did, I just didn't want to go away with him for the weekend."

August was so stunned he almost started stammering. "A—Away? Wh—where?"

"Orlando. Wayne has a time-share near Islands of Adventure."

"Orlando on the back of a Harley doesn't sound like your speed, Mom." And he didn't like the idea of her getting asked for sleepover dates.

But he didn't even want to think about that.

"It isn't." With a sigh, Beverly leaned back against the tan leather cushions of the couch and shook her head. "I just wish it would have lasted longer, you know? It was fun having plans. For the last four weeks, I had something to look forward to. A reason to get dressed up. I'm going to miss that feeling."

He knew what she meant. Two weeks had passed since he'd left DFW airport in a rush and flown home. Two weeks since either he or Evie had called or e-mailed. Two weeks since he'd thought he'd finally gotten the girl. "I'm sorry, Mom. I really am. That feeling stinks."

She sniffed. "It sure does." After wiping off a smudge of mascara under her eye, she looked him over a little more closely. "So, how are you doing?"

August shrugged. "All right."

"I doubt it."

He had to laugh at that. "Okay. I'm not doing so good, but I'll survive."

"I know you will." Repositioning herself on the couch, she tucked a leg underneath her. "Mike and Jan said Evie's working too hard again."

"I'm sure she is."

"They're worried about her."

He was, too. Evie gave so much of herself to others, she continually put herself last. Though he knew she'd dispute it to her dying day, Evie Ray needed someone in her life. Someone to make sure she remembered to smile. To make sure she remembered to take time for herself. For a while there, he'd been ready to take that job. "I hope she's okay."

"I thought the two of you were great together, dear."

"Thanks." Turning the conversation back to her, he admitted, "I never thought Wayne Peterson was the guy for you."

A wry smile lit her face. "I didn't think he was, either." Chuckling, she said, "Would you believe he hinted that Tanya needed braces again? I think he would have charged me, too."

August laughed. "Don't tell her that."

"I won't." Prodding a little bit more, she said, "You sure you don't think there's anything you can do to mend things with Evie?"

"We didn't get in a fight, Mom. She just doesn't want to try to make things work."

"She doesn't want to move."

"No, she doesn't. She doesn't want to visit, either."

"Oh, August."

"And though at first I really wanted her to move here,

after I heard her reasons, I promised myself I wouldn't ask her to move. What I really wanted was to be a part of her life."

"That wasn't asking too much."

"It was for her. She freaked out when Jenna broke her leg. She said she wouldn't have been able to deal with the guilt if she'd been here visiting me when that happened."

"It's understandable."

August said nothing.

"You know, I was always thankful that your dad had this resort. I liked him being home every night. We worked too hard, but we also had some great times. And we met so many wonderful people."

"And some not-so-nice people."

She laughed. "That, too. I don't know how we would have managed if he'd been a salesman or something and had to travel nonstop. It's hard raising children." Softening her voice, she said, "I don't envy Evie. That's a lot of responsibility on some very slim shoulders."

"She does okay." August stood up and went to the kitchen, picked up an apple and a knife and concentrated on peeling it into one long, straight line. "I never said she wasn't a good mother. She's a great mother."

"I'm just saying that I can't help but understand her side."

"The thing of it is, I think she could have really enjoyed living here. Her parents would have helped her, she could have worked with me, or at something else."

"You could have married her and taken care of her."

"I wanted to." He'd wanted to do more than that, though. He'd wanted to be by her side. To help her…and have her be there for him.

"Did you offer to move there?"

"Not really."

"But you could…don't you think?"

The question took him so much by surprise that he set down the knife before he cut himself. "Mom, remember the resort? Remember the unit troubles, the guests, the grounds maintenance?"

"Don't be pert with me, August."

"Then don't make it seem like I can just up and quit my job. And I certainly can't run this place from Texas, even if I wanted to, which I don't."

"You're being obtuse, and you're speaking like this place is made of flesh and bones."

"I'm talking facts here. Would you please join in?"

"The resort isn't a child. It might suffer a little when you're not there…but it will survive."

"Who's going to run it? Tanya? You?"

"Not me. There was a reason I had my dance studio. I never had the patience for people on vacation. But your sister will do a fine job…if you are willing to let her give it a try."

"Are you serious?"

"As a heart attack."

August winced. "Bad joke, Mom."

"Sorry, but I am being completely serious. My idea has merit, and I think you'd see that if you gave it a chance."

He knew she was right. Tanya was extremely capable. But the place seemed so much a part of him. Could he really just walk away from where he knew he was successful? Where there were memories of his dad at every corner?

"Think about it, August. Tanya's itching to have even more responsibility, and I think she'd do a good job of it."

"I know she would."

"Then isn't it time you stretched your wings a little, son? I mean, here you have the resort, but you're not happy. What do you want, August?" she asked softly. "This resort or Evie?"

Evie, his subconscious called out. But August didn't know if he was brave enough yet to listen to it.

"I've talked over the idea of running Silver Shells a little bit with Tanya. She and I could buy you out and then you would have the funds to start something new. Something on your own in Grapevine."

"It sounds like you two have talked this over more than just a little bit."

"We know you're happy when you're with Evie, August. It's natural for you two to want to be together."

They were back to that again. Just thinking about walking away from everything he'd known to a future in Texas made his mind spin. "There's no place like this in Grapevine."

"I don't imagine you'd want the same place. But maybe it's time to know something else? I was reading that Grapevine is making quite a name for itself as a conference destination. I wonder if there are many people who know how to run a conference center as well as you do."

Standing up, Beverly walked her empty teacup back into the kitchen. "Thanks for the tea, and for listening to me rattle on about Wayne, honey. I feel a lot better."

"I really am sorry things didn't work out with you and Dr. Peterson."

"I am, too, but maybe next time." She winked. "I've got a chat scheduled in a few hours. Maybe this gentleman will be the one."

He felt like thumping on the table. "You're going back to Harmonious Haven?"

"Of course. It's not the HH's fault that Wayne is in a hurry to get some action."

The whole idea was creepy. So uncomfortable,

August felt his cheeks heating, and he was sure he hadn't blushed since he'd walked in on Alison Sinclair taking a shower in Tanya's bathroom back in fourth grade. "But—"

"Love is a good thing, August. I loved your dad. I'd planned to spend the rest of my life by his side. Maybe I won't ever love again. But I won't know if I don't try, right? Time marches on."

With a small smile, she placed her hand over her heart. "Imagine how awful it would be if my heart gave out and I knew I had never tried?"

And with that, she took off, leaving August feeling like he'd completely misread his life. For almost thirty years, he'd been waiting for things to happen.

Methodically, he opened a few cabinets until he found a blank notebook and pulled out a pen, then headed to his computer. It was time to think about investing in Grapevine real estate. And, for the first time, a future with Evie.

"Momma, Missy's crying," Jenna said from the doorway.

Evie wearily leaned back in the kitchen chair and set down her teacup. "Thanks for letting me know." As a high-pitched wail echoed down the hallway, Evie figured her next-door neighbors knew Missy was crying, too.

"You gonna go get her?"

"I will in a second, hon," Evie said. Lord, had she ever been more tired? Missy had been fussy and sick for thirty-six hours straight, and Evie had been up for every single one of those minutes. There'd even been a few moments last night when Evie had joined her in the tearfest, though it hadn't helped to do much besides swell her eyes and bring on a raging headache.

Jenna looked worried, with her eyebrows scrunched up and her hands on her hips. "Momma, is she gonna be okay?"

"Uh-huh, the doctor said the pink medicine should kick in soon."

"You said that last night."

"Missy's ear hurts, Jenna. I'm doing everything I can. What more do you want?"

Jenna's eyes widened at Evie's sharp tone, and Evie sighed. "I'm sorry I snapped at you, honey," she said, enfolding her eldest in a little hug. "I'm just tired. Thanks for coming to get me. I'm glad you're so concerned."

"So we gonna go get her?"

"In a sec." As Missy cried some more, Evie walked to the stove, poured a little bit more hot water into her mug and followed Jenna into her bedroom, where she'd left Missy sleeping not twenty minutes earlier. There, Missy cried, her little body shaking with the force of her sobs.

Evie set down her teacup and scooped Missy into her arms, quickly checking her diaper to make sure the problem wasn't something easily solved. She held her close and leaned against the headboard. The new position seemed to ease Missy's pain, and the loud cries faded into sleepy whimpers.

Jenna kicked off her sandals and slipped into bed beside her. "She better now?"

"Not yet, but she will be soon, I bet. I gave her some aspirin about an hour ago."

Jenna glanced at the glowing green numbers on Evie's bedside table as Missy fussed and fumed. After the numbers clicked two times, she whispered, "Now?"

"Not yet."

"How much longer?"

Evie struggled to find the rest of her patience. "I don't know, baby."

"Maybe she needs Neena?"

"That's sweet, but I don't think she does." Patting the

pillow next to her, Evie said, "Want to come a little closer?"

"In a sec. I'm gonna go get one of my animals."

"You do that."

As Jenna disappeared, Evie cuddled Missy closer and glared at the phone.

It was Saturday and John was supposed to have the girls, but he'd called her on Thursday and said he had to go back to Japan.

She understood, but his absence made her feel even more alone. If he was in town, Evie knew he'd be offering to make a grocery run or at least take Jenna out for a movie.

Shoot, at this moment, she'd take almost anyone's help for an hour or two.

It didn't help that she had no one to blame for her independence but herself. Once again, she was working hard, attempting to do everything and cursing her stubborn pride for refusing to tell her parents or Sue or John that she was not okay.

But most of all, Evie truly regretted how she'd ended things with August.

Six weeks had gone by since that fateful conversation at the hospital and she'd sent him on his way. Six weeks with no calls or letters, e-mail messages or hearing his voice. Evie was enough of a realist to realize that she should've been more open-minded where he was concerned.

She should have admitted that the real reason she had run from August was that she didn't want to risk being pushed aside again.

She was afraid that one day August, like John, would discover that something in her was lacking.

There was room in her life for him. There had to be a

way to work things out. But because she still wasn't sure what that plan was, she'd steadfastly refused to give August a call.

And time had marched on. Jenna had been in a cast, then another one, then finally no cast at all. School had started, along with the dizzying round of soccer games, homework and parent meetings.

After a bunch of phone calls, her parents had decided against coming out before Halloween. Evie had breathed a sigh of relief. Work was stressful enough without hearing how her mother and dad wished she'd spend more time on herself.

Like she had another minute to spare in her life. Honestly, sometimes it seemed as if those idyllic days at Bishop's Gate had been a wonderful dream. Every once in a while, when Jenna and Missy were with John, Evie found herself opening up Jenna's plastic container of shells and just smelling them. Just so she'd remember what it felt like to have the sand under her feet.

Jenna came roaring back in just as Missy's eyes were drifting shut. "How's Missy?" she asked, attempting to keep her voice low.

Absently, Evie looked down. "Almost asleep," she whispered. "Maybe we can take a tiny nap, too."

Jenna lifted herself on the bed, dragging the stuffed golden retriever Evie had bought her just last week on up, too. "I'm tired. Missy kept me up all night."

"She kept me up, too. Earaches are no fun."

"No, ma'am."

Evie smiled at the response. Jenna's second grade teacher was old-school Texan, which meant just about every response needed to be peppered with *ma'am* and *sir.* The familiar words of respect made Evie think of her grandfather and serious conversations with her parents.

With a little heft, Evie placed Missy next to her, taking care to keep her head elevated a little bit, hoping that would help to alleviate the pain. Then, she scooted down and opened her arms to Jenna. "Want to cuddle?"

"Yes, Momma." Jenna giggled softly as she edged closer. Then, as only children seem to be able to do, she closed her eyes and fell promptly asleep.

Evie had just closed her eyes when the doorbell rang. What on earth?

Then she remembered. Two days ago, her parents called and mentioned that they'd found a cute basket on GIFTS.com that was filled to the brim with all kinds of fall harvest goodies. It must be delivery time.

Taking care not to budge either girl, Evie slid out of the bed. She approached the door, just as the doorbell rang again.

"Hold on," she said sharply, unlocking the padlock and pulling in the door to unlock the second set of locks. "If you wake up my baby, you're coming in and rocking her yourself, I don't care how many deliveries—"

"What deliveries?" August Meyer asked, as though he stood at her door every day.

A better woman than Evie would have something pretty and smart to say. Maybe would have summoned up a smile and a delighted welcome.

Evie had never been that kind of a girl. "What in the hell are you doing here?"

A slow smile, one just for her, spread across his face like wildfire. "I wanted to see you."

Feeling like a sledgehammer had just knocked her upside the head, Evie closed her eyes to still the pain. Here was the one man she'd dreamed about. The one man she'd never expected to see again. The one man she'd hoped she could mend things with, and start over again.

As his eyes raked over her, Evie felt as if he could see every new line on her face, every stain on her sweats. "Is now a bad time?"

Could there be a worse time? "It's not a good one. I…I look like the cat dragged me across the living room."

His lips twitched. "You do."

She covered her mouth with a hand. "I don't think I brushed my teeth today, either." When had she last brushed her teeth? Midnight?

"I brushed mine." And just to show how completely irresistible he was, he flashed his pearly whites.

No man should look so good. Holding herself upright against the door frame, she said, "Missy's sick. She's had a heck of an earache for three days."

Amusement faded as concern edged forward. "She okay?"

"No." Seeing that he had a rental car in her driveway, her curiosity was piqued further. "Would you like to come on in?"

"Only if you want me to."

She didn't know what she wanted. She wanted time to think. She wanted his arms around her. She wanted everything in her life to be easy.

Shoot. At the moment, a makeover or at least a clean T-shirt would be really appreciated. "Come on in."

He crossed into the entryway, closing the door behind him. Evie edged backward, afraid to touch him, because if she did, she'd grab hold of him in a death grip and never let him go. And he'd be grossed out and say something like he only stopped by because he'd forgotten his sunglasses or some such.

Scanning the living room, he said, "Where are the girls?"

"Asleep in my bed. We, um, were napping."

Dismay filled his gaze. "I'm sorry I woke you." Running a hand through his hair, he stepped back. "Look. How about I go find a room and you give me a phone call when you have time to talk?"

"You'd do that? You'd leave and sit and wait for me to call?"

He smiled a little sadly. "Yeah. I've, uh, been waiting a long time for you, Evie. I can wait a little longer."

A knot formed in her throat, making it difficult to swallow. She searched for words. To find the right thing to say. Because one thing was for sure: she couldn't do it anymore.

Couldn't pretend she didn't want him.

Couldn't pretend she didn't want a future with August.

Couldn't pretend that she hadn't fallen in love.

Finally she said, "I'm sorry I sent you away."

He pursed his lips. "Ev—"

"I'm sorry I didn't call and apologize," she interrupted in a rush. "I'm sorry for a whole lot of things. I'm sorry I didn't just tell you that I was afraid to grab hold of you, just in case one day you didn't want me anymore."

"That will never happen."

He sounded so sure, so August-like, Evie knew in a flash that he was telling her the truth. For better or worse, August wanted her. "I believe you," she whispered. Then, just when she thought her face couldn't look any worse, the tears came running. Hastily, she rubbed her face. "Sorry."

In two steps, he was at her side. "Hush now, Evie. Please don't cry."

"I'm trying not to."

"Everything's going to be okay," he murmured, folding her against him, rubbing his cheek against the top of her head.

Like a really good dream, all things August surrounded her right away, making the world seem a little brighter, her life seem a little easier.

And the words she knew she had to say came a little faster. "I broke your heart and mine when I asked you to leave at the hospital. As soon as I got home and really thought about things, I knew I'd been wrong, but I was too afraid to change in order to make things better. I don't know why."

"I do," he murmured, pressing his lips to her brow. "You were thinking for the both of us."

"Was I?" She lifted her head back enough to catch his expression. "I don't think I've ever been that thoughtful in my life."

He chuckled. "That's where you're wrong, Evie. Only a mother who loved her kids would put their needs first. Only a woman who'd had her heart broken would worry about it being trampled again. I could never fault you for that."

"But I should have listened to what you said."

"And I should have been more stubborn and never left Dallas without patching things up." Looking into her eyes, he said, "I should have tried harder."

So many mixed-up emotions were running through her, Evie felt as if her head was about to explode. "I gotta sit down."

"Me, too." Taking her hand, August led her to the couch, and to her delight, kept right on holding that hand when he sat by her side. "Will you listen to what I have to say?"

"I'll listen. I'm too stunned to talk."

"I realize that all my life, I've been really good at waiting. Taking the easy way. I always planned on taking over the resort. I knew how to do that, and accepted it. I'm ashamed to say I never even considered another path for my life."

Thinking of Bishop's Gate, of Silver Shells, she said, "You had a good path."

"After the pregnancy thing, when everything turned out okay, I still wanted a future with you."

Had she ever really told him that she'd just been scared and running? "August—"

"Hold on. When you went to A&M for college, I wanted you to go to Florida State. When you said no, I didn't even consider transferring. It never even crossed my mind. I was so confused—you sounded so happy that we didn't have to get married. That there was nothing keeping us together. So, I just decided to wait some more for you."

"And then I met John and didn't go back to Florida."

August looked at his hands. "And I let you move on without a fight. Evie, I've regretted that more times than I can count. But I'm done waiting." With resolve shining in those green eyes she knew so well, he took her hands. "Evie, I'm not going to sit and wait any longer."

She was afraid to hope. "What are you saying?"

"I came out here a few days ago and looked at commercial properties with a Realtor…with Terri, actually. Between the two of us, I think I found a place to buy."

"Huh?"

"I'm going to take over the old Wyndmark Hotel and update it. I'm going to run it."

"August?" Maybe it was the lack of sleep. Maybe it was too many hours of hearing Jenna talk about Dora the Explorer that made her unable to relate to real conversation.

Maybe what he was saying sounded too good to be true.

"I'm going to move here, Evie. To Grapevine. I want to move here and spend my life with you."

"You'd be willing to do that?" she whispered. "You'd be willing to leave Bishop's Gate? Silver Shells?" She gasped. "Your mom and her heart?"

A slow smile appeared on his lips. "My mother very snippily reminded me that she and her heart are doing just fine, thank you very much. She also took the time to remind me that life was meant for living, not wishing."

Moving closer, gazing at her gently, August said, "Will you marry me, Evie? Live with me here in Texas?"

Her whole world collapsed. Well, the world that she knew, where she was tired and alone. Worried and stressed.

In its place was a little bit of sunshine, and its name was August Meyer. She closed her eyes and recalled that long walk with her father, when she'd confided to him that August made her *feel.* Over and over, he made her feel good and attractive and worthwhile.

And, after all these years…he was doing it again.

No one else had ever made her feel so good. No one else had ever done so much for her and asked for so little.

"Are you sure you want to do this? The girls…John?"

"I want to be with you. With the girls." With a lopsided smile, he added, "I couldn't care less about John."

Evie's lips twitched. "I can live with that. You sure you know what you're getting into? Missy's no piece of cake when she's sick. Jenna's not easy on her best day."

"I don't want easy. I'm not asking for that. I just want us to be together." Taking her hand, he said, "I'll hold Missy when she's sick. I'll hold your hand when Jenna and toy cell phones drive you nuts. I want to be by your side."

His words meant everything. Without saying it, August was promising he'd never leave her. He'd be her partner through thick and thin.

Could she hope for so much?

"I want us, Evie. I want it all. I want everything."

She still couldn't believe it. "But the beach—"

He groaned. "Evie, answer me, dammit! I'm going crazy waiting for you to answer me."

"I'm warning you now, August Meyer, if I say yes, I'll mean it forever."

"If you say yes, I'll be the happiest man in the world."

What was really crazy was Evie was certain August meant those words. She meant everything to him…just as he meant everything to her.

And because it all made such perfect sense, Evie Ray finally gave in. "Yes."

Triumph lit those green eyes of his. And just as he was about to lean in and get up close and personal, Evie remembered just how grubby she was. Hastily, she jumped to her feet. "Stay here. You're not kissing me like this."

"I don't care."

"Oh, I do."

August flopped against the couch as she headed back to her bedroom. "Evie Ray, you'd try the patience of a saint."

"Thank goodness you're not a saint, August Meyer. Thank goodness you're just you."

And with that, Evie ran to the bathroom to splash some much-needed water on her face, brush her teeth and get ready to see August again.

It wasn't an exaggeration to say she could hardly wait.

Epilogue

"Nobody move," Mike Ray announced from his spot behind the camera on the tripod.

Assembled in the snug cottage's living room, Evie and the rest of the family groaned.

"Do you even know how to work that, Dad?" Ben called out, ignoring Mike's orders and shifting his stance. "I haven't seen any lights blinking. Did you remember to put the batteries in?"

Evie bit back a smile. Her brother never had been able to hold his tongue. Back in junior high, it had gotten him grounded at least once a week. Now, however, Evie noticed that their parents could hardly hold back their expressions of amusement.

"They're in."

"You sure?"

"Benjamin!"

"Yes, ma'am."

"Go back to how you were, Ben," their dad muttered. "You've gone and messed everything up. Now I can't see Tanya."

"Yeah, move, Ben," Tanya said from over his left shoulder.

He ignored his dad again and turned completely around. "You're sure bossy for a sister-in-law."

Mike yelled, "Ben!"

Ben faced front again.

August rolled his eyes. "You don't know bossy until you've met the Ray family. Every one of you—from the youngest to the oldest—thinks he or she knows best."

"I heard that, August," Evie said.

"Me, too," Jenna said.

"Good. 'Cause I meant it."

"Move to the left," Mike called out. "Oh, shoot. Now we can't see Evie at all."

"Is that a problem?" Ben said, ever the joker.

"Shut up, Ben," August said with a laugh, hugging Evie closer. "No wonder they don't let you out of the army very often. How's this, Mike?"

"Good, but now—"

"Oh, for heavens sakes! Take the picture, Mike!" Jan said. "I've got to go check my cookies before they burn."

"Hold your horses."

Jenna laughed. "There's no horses here!"

"Daddy, take the picture, please," Evie shouted. "Missy's getting heavy."

"I'll hold her, Ev," August offered. "Hand her over."

"Don't you move a muscle, Evie. Nobody move," Mike commanded in such a tone that even Ben didn't dare crack a joke. "Fine. One, two, three," he bellowed, running into place. Everyone did their best to move into position, but as the camera flashed once, then twice more, Evie had a feeling that this year's picture was going to be the craziest one ever.

Finally it was done.

"Relax and stand aside!" her mother called out. "My cookies are about to burn."

Like bees in a fire, they all dispersed in a heartbeat.

All except for Evie and August. "I'm so glad we're here for Christmas," she said, meaning every word. She'd been looking forward to returning to their special place from the moment August had suggested they drop everything and go.

"Me, too," August said, smiling as Jenna ordered Ben around. "Christmas wouldn't be the same without extreme chaos. Are you sad we can only stay for five days? I just couldn't make Craig do everything on his own for longer than that."

"I think five days is fine," Evie said, looking at the pretty, artificial tree her parents had in the family room. "I love being here, but I'll be kind of excited to spend New Year's alone with you."

After they'd gotten married the month before, she, August, John and Terri had discussed holidays and calendars. Thankfully, everyone was able to get along amicably.

And because they all loved the girls, both couples blocked out time on their calendars with them. Therefore, John was getting the girls for New Year's while she got them for the whole week surrounding Christmas.

Seeing that Missy and Jenna were just fine with all their relatives, August pulled Evie outside, into the dunes and the warm, balmy temperatures.

Unable to help herself, Evie breathed deep, loving the scent of the sand and ocean surrounding her. Loving the breath of wind that coaxed her hair into gentle waves around her shoulders.

She slid off her sandals as August wrapped her up in his arms. "You make me happy, Evie," he murmured, kissing her lightly. "Hey, have I told you today?"

"Truth?"

He held up a pinky. "Always."

She widened her eyes and lied through her teeth. "No."

Surprise, then an amused glint, entered his expression. "It's five o'clock in the evening and I've let almost the day go by without telling you I love you? Really?"

"Really." She tilted her chin up flirtatiously. "I'm shocked, you know. I expected better from my husband."

"Evie Meyer, you're lying! You're lying on a pinky promise."

And with that, August tackled Evie into the sand and kissed her senseless. When they came up for air, he brushed his lips to her brow. "I love you. I always have. I always will."

Against her will, Evie felt tears prick her eyes. He'd said those same words on their wedding day, and the same three promises every day since.

She still couldn't believe she was so lucky.

"I love you, too," she murmured, just as he was about to kiss her again.

And as his lips claimed hers, and she felt the warm sand under her back and August's solid form sprawled against hers, Evie realized that everything was going to be just fine.

And that she would never, ever be lonely again.

New York Times bestselling author

DIANA PALMER

Handsome, eligible ranch owner Stuart York knew
Ivy Conley was too young for him, so he closed his heart
to her and sent her away—despite the fireworks between
them. Now, years later, Ivy is determined not to be
treated like a little girl anymore…but for some reason,
Stuart is always fighting her battles for her. And safe in
Stuart's arms makes Ivy feel like a woman…his woman.

Winter Roses

Available November.

www.eHarlequin.com

HRIBC03985

Romantic
SUSPENSE

**Sparked by Danger,
Fueled by Passion.**

Onyxx agent Sully Paxton's only chance of
survival lies in the hands of his enemy's daughter
Melita Krizova. He doesn't know he's a pawn in the
beautiful island girl's own plan for escape. Can
they survive their ruses and their fiery attraction?

*Look for the next installment in the
Spy Games miniseries,*

Sleeping with Danger
by Wendy Rosnau

Available November 2007 wherever you buy books.

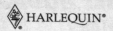

INTRIGUE

WHITEHORSE MONTANA

Love can be blind...and deadly

On the night of her best friend's wedding, Laci Cavanaugh
saw that something just didn't seem right with Alyson's
new husband. When she heard the news of Alyson's
"accidental" death on her honeymoon, Laci was positive
that it was no accident at all....

Look for

THE MYSTERY MAN OF WHITEHORSE

BY B.J. DANIELS

*Available November
wherever you buy books.*

www.eHarlequin.com

HI69291

REQUEST YOUR FREE BOOKS!
2 FREE NOVELS PLUS 2
FREE GIFTS!

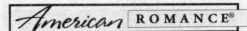

American ROMANCE®

Heart, Home & Happiness!

YES! Please send me 2 FREE Harlequin American Romance® novels and my 2 FREE gifts. After receiving them, if I don't wish to receive any more books, I can return the shipping statement marked "cancel." If I don't cancel, I will receive 4 brand-new novels every month and be billed just $4.24 per book in the U.S., or $4.99 per book in Canada, plus 25¢ shipping and handling per book and applicable taxes, if any*. That's a savings of close to 15% off the cover price! I understand that accepting the 2 free books and gifts places me under no obligation to buy anything. I can always return a shipment and cancel at any time. Even if I never buy another book from Harlequin, the two free books and gifts are mine to keep forever.

154 HDN EEZK   354 HDN EEZV

Name	(PLEASE PRINT)

Address		Apt. #

City	State/Prov.	Zip/Postal Code

Signature (if under 18, a parent or guardian must sign)

Mail to the **Harlequin Reader Service®**:
IN U.S.A.: P.O. Box 1867, Buffalo, NY 14240-1867
IN CANADA: P.O. Box 609, Fort Erie, Ontario L2A 5X3

Not valid to current Harlequin American Romance subscribers.

Want to try two free books from another line?
Call 1-800-873-8635 or visit www.morefreebooks.com.

* Terms and prices subject to change without notice. NY residents add applicable sales tax. Canadian residents will be charged applicable provincial taxes and GST. This offer is limited to one order per household. All orders subject to approval. Credit or debit balances in a customer's account(s) may be offset by any other outstanding balance owed by or to the customer. Please allow 4 to 6 weeks for delivery.

Your Privacy: Harlequin is committed to protecting your privacy. Our Privacy Policy is available online at www.eHarlequin.com or upon request from the Reader Service. From time to time we make our lists of customers available to reputable firms who may have a product or service of interest to you. If you would prefer we not share your name and address, please check here. ☐

HAR07

Cut from the soap opera that made her a star, America's
TV goddess Gloria Hart heads back to her childhood
home to regroup. But when a car crash maroons her in
small-town Mississippi, it's local housewife Jenny Miller
to the rescue. Soon these two very different women,
together with Gloria's sassy assistant, become fast friends,
realizing that they bring out a certain secret something
in each other that men find irresistible!

Look for

THE SECRET
GODDESS CODE

by

PEGGY WEBB

Available November wherever you buy books.

HARLEQUIN®

NeXt™

TheNextNovel.com

HN88146

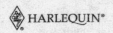

EVERLASTING LOVE™

Every great love has a story to tell™

Charlie fell in love with Rose Kaufman
before he even met her, through stories her
husband, Joe, used to tell. When Joe is killed
in the trenches, Charlie helps Rose through
her grief and they make a new life together.
But for Charlie, a question remains—can
love be as true the second time around?
Only one woman can answer that....

Look for

The Soldier and the Rose

by

Linda Barrett

Available November wherever you buy books.

www.eHarlequin.com

HEL65421

HARLEQUIN®

Mediterranean
N I G H T S™

Not everything is above board
on Alexandra's Dream!

Enjoy plenty of secrets, drama and sensuality
in the latest from Mediterranean Nights.

Coming in November 2007...

BELOW DECK

by

Dorien Kelly

Determined to protect her young son,
widow Mei Lin Wang keeps him hidden
aboard *Alexandra's Dream* under cover of
her job. But life gets extremely complicated
when the ship's security officer, Gideon Dayan,
is piqued by the mystery surrounding this
beautiful, haunted woman....

www.eHarlequin.com   HM38965

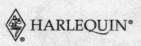

HARLEQUIN®

American ROMANCE®

COMING NEXT MONTH

#1185 THE PERFECT TREE by Roz Denny Fox, Ann DeFee and Tanya Michaels
There's something magical about sitting in front of a roaring fire, breathing in the rich sights and smells of a beautifully decorated Christmas tree. This holiday season, join three of your favorite Harlequin American Romance authors in three stories about finding love at a special time of year—and about finding the perfect Christmas tree.

#1186 DOWN HOME CAROLINA CHRISTMAS by Pamela Browning
Carrie Smith has seen her share of clunkers drive into her gas station in Yewville, South Carolina, but never has anything like movie star Luke Mason in his Ferrari shown up at the pump. And no matter how hard the sexy movie star tries to persuade her otherwise, she's positive Hollywood and Hicksville will never meet!

#1187 CHRISTMAS AT BLUE MOON RANCH by Lynnette Kent
Major Daniel Trent came to south Texas to be a rancher, although Willa Mercado doubts the injured veteran can handle the physical challenges of the life. She bets he'll back out of buying part of her ranch before their three-month agreement is up. But Daniel has every intention of spending Christmas—and the rest of his life—with Willa and her kids at Blue Moon.

#1188 ALL I WANT FOR CHRISTMAS by Ann Roth
Tina Morrell has her hands full when a dear family friend needs her help just as Tina's career in the cutthroat world of advertising takes off. But there's a surprise waiting for her back home on Halo Island—a single dad and a little girl who want to show her what the holiday season is really about....

www.eHarlequin.com

HARCNM1007